ISLAND

FORTRESS

PETER TONNA

ISBN: 978-1-7638029-0-2 (ebook)
ISBN: 978-1-7638029-1-9 (paperback)
ISBN: 978-1-7638029-2-6 (hardback)

A literary work of Poete Books

poetebooks@gmail.com
www.poete.com.au/books

CONTENTS

Illustrations 4

INTRODUCTION 7

PROLOGUE 15

DREAMERS 17

THE DECLARATION 23

FIRST STRIKE 29

WAR ROOM SORROW 37

RELIEF 45

ONE HUNDRED DAYS 51

THE EMPIRE STRIKES BACK 55

A HAPPIER YEAR? 61

THE LUFTWAFFE 67

HOLDING ON 77

A NEW SEASON 83

THEY RETURN 89

THE DOWNPOUR 97

Il-MIRAKLU TAL-BOMBA 107

HELP! 117

THE LAST HOPE 125

ENGULFED 133

OHIO MIRACLE 145

FOR GALLANTRY 157

THE TIDE TURNS 169

END IN SIGHT 173

TINY BRIGHT FLAME 179

EPILOGUE 187

Bibliography 195

Illustrations

1. Map of Malta (source: Map by Free Vector Maps; https://freevectormaps.com/malta/MT-EPS-01-0001?ref=atr. Edited by Peter Tonna).
2. Map of Valletta and Grand Harbour (source: Peter Tonna).
3. The Gloster Gladiator biplane 'Faith' restored on display at the Malta War Museum, Valletta. Presented to the Maltese people by the Royal Air Force. (source: Alamy Stock Photo).
4. Memorial dedicated to the first casualties of the war on Malta on Fort St. Elmo. The inscription: 'These six men were the first soldiers to die in Malta in the Second World War'; 'Killed in action on this very spot at 7:45 am 11 June 1940' (source: Peter Tonna).
5. Lascaris War Rooms: main control room. Preserved as a museum in Valletta (source: Alamy Stock Photo).
6. The damaged ship bell of HMS *Illustrious*, which survived the blitz in January 1941 (source: Malta War Museum, Valletta; Peter Tonna).
7. Bomb damage in Valletta: a heavily damaged street in Valletta, Malta. On the right, the cherished Opera House destroyed (source: Alamy Stock Photo).
8. Mosta Basilica (source: Petar Avramoski, Unsplash).
9. Mosta Dome from the inside. Considered the fourth-largest unsupported dome in the world (third in Europe); 2.7 metres shorter in diameter than the dome of St. Peter's Basilica in Rome (source: Joshua Kettle, Unsplash).
10. *Ohio* tanker before being fitted for Operation Pedestal (source: Hagley Museum & Library).
11. European map of control; mid-1942. Map shows Malta completely isolated: Gibraltar and Egypt the closest Allied support. The Axis area includes the puppet territories (source: Peter Tonna).
12. Operation Pedestal: The operation begins. An aerial view of some of the ships escorting the convoy. In the forefront:

aircraft carriers HMS *Eagle*, HMS *Indomitable* and HMS *Victorious* (source: Alamy Stock Photo).

13. Operation Pedestal: The tanker *Ohio* under heavy attack (source: Alamy Stock Photo).
14. Operation Pedestal: Sailors watch HMS *Eagle* sinking after being torpedoed (source: Alamy Stock Photo).
15. Operation Pedestal: The *Brisbane Star* sails into the Grand Harbour (source: Alamy Stock Photo).
16. Operation Pedestal: The sinking tanker *Ohio*, held up by Navy destroyers, making its way to the mouth of the Grand Harbour, navigating the mine fields (source: Alamy Stock Photo).
17. Operation Pedestal: The damaged tanker *Ohio*, supported by Navy destroyers, limping into the Grand Harbour after an epic voyage across the western Mediterranean (source: Alamy Stock Photo).
18. Siege Bell War Memorial in Valletta: monument dedicated to those who died during the siege of Malta in the Second World War (source: Alamy Stock Photo).
19. The nameboard of *Ohio* (source: Malta War Museum, Valletta; Peter Tonna).
20. The George Cross Medal awarded to the island in April 1942 (source: Malta War Museum, Valletta; Peter Tonna).
21. The letter written by the King that accompanied the George Cross Medal (source: Malta War Museum, Valletta; Peter Tonna).

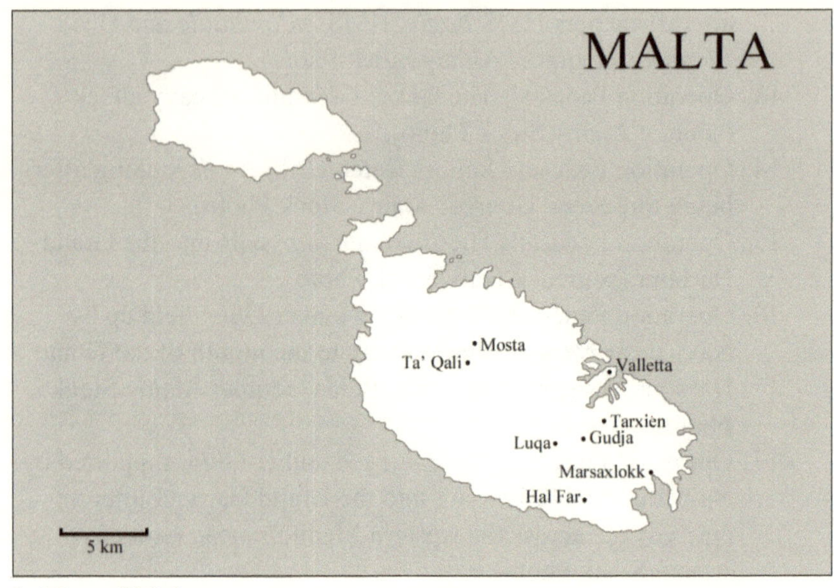

1. Map of Malta

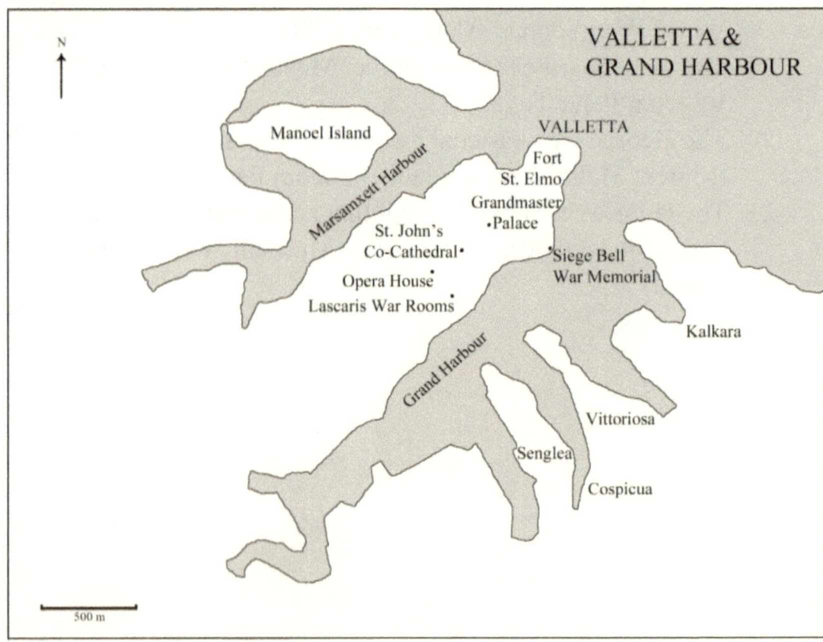

2. Map of Valletta and Grand Harbour.

INTRODUCTION

Malta is a small island nation of 316 square kilometres. The mainland is 27 kilometres long and 14.5 kilometres wide. It is approximately one-third the size of Berlin, one-quarter the size of Rome and one-fifth the size of London. Malta sits in the middle of the Mediterranean Sea in close proximity to Sicily to the north, Tunisia to the west and Libya to the south. The island has been a strategically vital piece of land since ancient times and has provided a place of respite for seafarers throughout history. Due to the location and natural rock formation and foundation, the island has been highly desirable for any would-be conqueror in the region. As history reveals, Malta would be the scene of many battles and sieges over its long history; the prehistoric temples on the island indicate that the earliest known signs of civilisation date as far back as approximately 3,500 BC.[1]

One of the better known battles for Malta occurred in 1565, known as the Great Siege of Malta. The Knights Hospitaller, also known as the Knights of St. John, made Malta their base in 1530 after being driven out of Rhodes by the invading Ottomans. Under the rule of Suleiman the Magnificent, the Ottomans were commanded to take Malta. This set the scene for what many historians have described as one of the most gruesome battles of the sixteenth century. The Ottoman Empire desired Malta for its strategic location: to set up a base to launch an attack against the rest of Europe, beginning with Sicily. But the Knights, with the unwavering determination of the Maltese people – despite being outnumbered six-to-one – would not

---

[1] https://whc.unesco.org/en/list/132/

surrender the island easily. Malta's resistance led the Ottomans to resort to gaining control of the island by force. Due to Malta's naturally high cliffs and rocky shoreline, the only reasonable location for invasion was the Grand Harbour. The Ottomans captured Fort St. Elmo but were repelled from advancing further inland, confined to the Grand Harbour area. The Maltese hardly matched the military might and power of the Ottomans, but they persisted. Following four months of savage warfare, enduring over 130,000 cannonballs, the Knights and the Maltese people prevented the Ottoman invaders gaining control of Malta. The Ottomans, struggling with disease and wearied by the Maltese people's incessant will, eventually retreated. It is estimated that the Ottomans lost over 25,000 men, three times the casualties of those fighting for Malta. It became a famous victory, not only for Malta but also for Europe, which was already under partial control of the Ottoman Empire and on the verge of collapse. The triumph provided a source of hope for the rest of Europe – that the seemingly invincible powerhouse could indeed be conquered. The Ottomans rarely met opposition they could not overpower; however, the resilience, fortitude and heart of the Maltese people, despite the odds against them, withstood all the Ottomans could throw at them.

In another act of resistance against an invading party, Napoleon Bonaparte's reign over Malta lasted only two years. His stringent regime and policies incited the people to revolt, with the help of the British, the French surrendered in 1800. The Maltese people accepted British rule, beginning a longstanding relationship – lasting 164 years until Malta gained independence in 1964 – of mutual respect and recognition that worked well for both entities. The island had a military power as its protector, while the British Empire possessed a Mediterranean base of strategic importance.

A new era for the Maltese people began in 1814 when the island officially became a British Crown Colony. Although under British rule, unlike other colonies, Malta was granted self-governance and its inhabitants sought to maintain their own identity as a culture and people group. Historically, Malta has had strong ties with Italy; the Norman Conquest in the eleventh century had established Malta as part of the kingdom of Sicily. Although the Norman occupation only lasted a little over 100 years, an association endured between Malta and Italy for centuries. The Italian language was spoken widely, particularly in government, commerce, culture and education. It was not until the mid-1930s that the Maltese government declared Maltese and English the official languages of Malta.

As a new decade neared, the future identity of Malta and its people once again entered a period of uncertainty. The Italian government were implementing plans to reunify lands once considered a part of the Italian Kingdom, while rumours of war on mainland Europe were growing. For Malta, an ever-increasing threat loomed from the north; as time would tell, the island nation would soon endure the most demanding battle in its long history.

∞

It has been suggested that the First World War did not really end but rather dimmed to a standoff. The seeds of discontent were sown shortly after the peace treaties were signed. The Treaty of Versailles blamed, primarily, Germany for the conflict. The victorious powers, mainly France, ravaged Germany, claiming portions of their land and imposing crushing compensations; their economy decimated, the German people lost their savings and livelihoods and were plunged into poverty. Sanctions were also imposed upon the Austro-Hungarian Empire, while the Ottoman Empire was broken up and divided between the British and the French: all ingredients comprising the foundations of the rise of nationalism.

In 1922, Benito Mussolini became leader of Italy. His Fascist Party held to an extreme ideology, including grand ambitions to make Italy a supreme world power. In his first few years of rule, Mussolini's concerns were domestic policy and entrenching his power base. In the mid-1930s, he began to wield his power outside of Italy. Malta was in his sights, to be included as part of a new Roman Empire along with the region of the northern Mediterranean coast to northern Africa. Italy had already held control of Libya since 1911 and had plans to annex Egypt and Sudan from British control.

In Germany, the leader of a small political party, the National Socialist German Workers' Party, known as the Nazis, began to make his mark in the political arena. Adolf Hitler, an ex–First World War soldier, attempted a coup to overthrow the government in 1923. However, he failed and was incarcerated for nine months. Despite this, the German people were drawn to Hitler and his passionate orations. He realised that, in order to rise to power, he must take the legitimate, legal route rather than use force. It would take Hitler ten years to fulfil his political aspirations.

In January of 1933, Adolf Hitler becomes Chancellor of Germany. In the following year, he becomes the supreme ruler of Germany following the death of President Hindenburg. Hitler's rise to power, which began in the early 1920s, is now complete. He has grand visions of restoring Germany to global prominence, to build a new Reich that would stand for a thousand years; and now, with all the power at his disposal, he is willing to use force. Hitler withdraws Germany from the League of Nations pact – an international organisation created after the First World War ended to maintain world peace – after the other signatories denied his request to increase the size of Germany's military forces. He increases the size of the German Army to 300,000 men. In 1935, Germany enforces military service and establishes a German air force: the Luftwaffe. Three powerful dictators now hold considerable rank in Europe: Mussolini, Hitler and Joseph Stalin of the Union of Soviet Socialist Republics (USSR).

In 1935, Italy invades Abyssinia (Ethiopia).

In 1936, German forces reoccupy the Rhineland, a buffer zone annexed by France as part of the Treaty of Versailles. Hitler and Mussolini form an alliance, the Berlin–Rome Axis. Japan, with its own aspirations to dominance, invades China. Japan would join the Axis in 1940. Ultimately, the Axis alliance recognised German dominion over continental Europe, Italian dominion over the Mediterranean and Japanese dominion over Asia and the Pacific. Until the late 1930s, Britain and France had been considered Europe's major military powers; however, the balance of power was wholly altered by the Axis alliance.

Germany's advance throughout mainland Europe is rapid. In 1938, Germany invades Austria without resistance, declaring unification with Germany.

Hitler desires to annex the predominantly German ethnic region of Sudetenland, which was part of Czechoslovakia at that time. The Allied powers of Britain and France seek to avoid conflict via diplomatic means. The British Prime Minister, Neville Chamberlain, meets with Hitler in Germany and agrees to terms regarding the matter; the British and French leaders would not impede Hitler's annexation of Sudetenland, on the assurance that Sudetenland would be the last of Hitler's territorial claims. One month later, Hitler demands that the Polish region of Danzig be restored to Germany. In 1939, the Germans take control of the rest of Czechoslovakia, giving the region of Ruthenia to Hungary, one of Germany's allies. The British and the French realise that they cannot trust Hitler's word and began to see Germany as a serious threat to the stability of Europe. The Allies declare their support for Poland and threaten Germany with war should they invade Danzig. Meanwhile, Mussolini makes his own territorial advances, annexing Albania. The USSR and Germany enter into a non-aggression pact. One of the terms of the pact is that Poland be split between Germany and the USSR. This was a serious threat to both the Allied powers and Poland maintaining its autonomy. At the start of September, the Germans attack Poland from the air, then by land. Swiftly, they capture Danzig and set their sights on the capital, Warsaw. Polish forces do their best to resist German advances. Allied forces demand that the Germans withdraw from Poland. However, the Germans do not comply; as a result, Britain and France (along with Australia and New Zealand) officially enter the war on 3 September – the beginning of the Second World War. South Africa and Canada join the Allies within the following week. At this point, the United States of America (USA) maintains its neutrality. By the end of September, Poland collapses in the face of German forces and Hitler seeks peaceful terms with Britain and France. However, the Allies reject Hitler's request for peace; so Hitler orders attacks on the West to begin, beginning with a bombing raid on Britain on 16 October. In the following months, minor battles ensue: aerial combat, bombing raids and tit-for-tat exchange of fire. Although the war has begun, these skirmishes are only a shadow of what is to come.

By the end of 1939, Germany has amassed an army of 1,500,000 men and considerably bolstered its military arsenal to surpass that of Britain and France combined. Italy has also bolstered its military capability to become a military power, with modern air and impressive naval fleets. However, Britain remains the supreme naval force in Europe. Amidst the ongoing clashes, at the start of 1940, Hitler sets his sights on Western Europe and draws plans for attack. In April, despite previously declaring neutrality, Hitler invades Norway and Denmark, a tactical move that would provide a northern base from which Germany could attack Britain as well as securing the Norwegian coastline, especially the port of Narvik, through which Sweden's high-grade iron ore passes – of which both Britain and Germany are consumers. Denmark surrenders the day following Germany's invasion. Norway would prove a tougher task; a fierce battle breaks out between the British Royal Navy and German forces. Initially, the Royal Navy were able to halt German progress, inflicting several losses. However, by 13 April, German forces occupy the capital, Oslo; Allied forces surround them. Over several weeks, the Germans launch a counterattack and are able to halt the Allied advancement. By late May, Allied forces learn of key developments on mainland Europe. Germany has invaded France, Luxemburg, Holland and Belgium. By the end of the first week in June, Allied forces evacuate Norway, considering it a less important frontier – but the Norwegians fight on.

During Germany's advance through mainland Europe, British Prime Minister Neville Chamberlain resigns and is replaced by Winston Churchill. On 15 May, Holland surrenders while battles ensue throughout northern France and Belgium. Allied forces lose ground quickly and, by the end of May, the King of Belgium orders his troops to surrender and Allied forces retreat to the shores of Dunkirk. The concentration of hundreds of thousands of British, French and Belgian personnel surrounded by German troops, in an open area, leaves them vulnerable to attack. An operation to rescue the soldiers takes effect, called Operation Dynamo. British civilians play an integral role in rescuing stranded troops, using their own personal sea vessels, lifeboats, yachts, fishing boats and rowboats. They depart British ports over fifty kilometres away and evacuate the stranded soldiers, making multiple trips. Dunkirk's port facilities were destroyed by the Luftwaffe, meaning that the soldiers had to be rescued from the beaches, making the operation even more difficult. However, in one week, over 330,000 British and French soldiers were taken safely back to Britain. The last rescue ship leaves the shores of Dunkirk on 4 June. The success of the operation was largely due to the British Royal Air Force (RAF) presence over France and Belgium to deter German bombers from attacking Allied soldiers.

∞

Malta had prepared for the worst over the years. In the mid-1930s, a policy was implemented to carve out shelters in the soft limestone rock on which the island's infrastructure is built. This policy proved instrumental in minimising civilian casualties during the war. In the late 1930s, as conflict began throughout Europe, the Maltese government detained suspected pro-Italian sympathisers. Italians working in Malta were sent back to their homeland. Blackout and air raid drills were held, curfews were practised, and volunteers were sought to defend the countryside. At the beginning of the Second World War, the population of Malta was approximately 280,000, most of the population living in or within a short radius of the Grand Harbour and Valletta, the capital.

The Axis powers' quest for world domination initiated the largest conflict the world – and indeed humanity – had ever seen. Malta, a tiny island nation, would prove to be a spanner in the giant cogs of the Axis war machine. Not by power, not by might, but by sheer perseverance against the odds, an enduring hope and a series of astonishing events, the Maltese would endure. Just like Malta became the hope for Europe in the Great Siege of 1565, it again became the hope, not only for Europe, but for the whole world …

PROLOGUE

Rita and her close-knit group of friends enter a new decade of possibilities. Their schooling years behind them, on the cusp of adulthood, they ponder the next phase of their lives. Living day by day in these gap years, little do they know that the distant horizon is fraught with uncertainly and struggle; the surrounding conflict would reach their shores and thrust them into a situation they would never choose to be in.

This group has known one another since they were pre-teens; they all completed their schooling two years ago. Louie Borg, Helena Spiteri, Maria Farrugia, Joe Caruana and Rita Schembri. Of the five, Joe and Rita share a unique bond, having known each other since their very first day of little school; their families have been close friends ever since.

Louie has been a feature of his mother's bakery since he could crawl. The only times he was not there was while he attended school; otherwise, he is assisting his mother to bake and exploring his own passion, creating new and bold sweet and savoury treats. Helena adores children and cares for them profoundly. She never really left school; after finishing her studies, she simply changed roles from student to teacher's help: the first step towards becoming a teacher, following in the footsteps of her favourite aunt. Maria's family is wealthier than most. Always given nice gifts growing up, she became accustomed to opulence and has grand desires to continue living as such. Her father, a bank manager, gives her a fortnightly stipend, which she is saving to go to the southern coast of France one day. Joe works part time at the dockyards. When he is not working, he is volunteering wherever there is need; he has an innate drive to help his fellow man and is currently volunteering at the hospital.

Rita, seventeen years old, lives with her parents in the quaint town of Mosta. Months prior to the war reaching Malta, she took on a casual administration role in the Lascaris War Rooms, otherwise known as the Command Headquarters beneath Valletta, where her father is a high-ranking officer in the Maltese Command. It is a fill-in job while she figures out her future, which remains uncertain. The one thing she is sure of is her passion for the written word; an avid writer, she has maintained a journal entry every day since she was given a diary on her tenth birthday.

This next phase of her life will force her to confront the very depths of her emotions, experiences and perceptions of both herself and the world around her, her journal entries documenting the most raw and visceral feelings she has ever experienced – of the days that will transform her life, her family, her friends and her country … forever.

DREAMERS

Journal entry: 2 June 1940

I cherish days like today, meeting close friends somewhere picturesque. The sun's gleam was spectacularly bright, reflecting off the rich yellow sand. I understand why this place is called Golden Bay. The cool westerly Mediterranean breeze the perfect complement to ease the simmering heat of the afternoon. The pristine emerald water caressed the sparkling shoreline, providing a soothing soundtrack, mixed with the intermittent laughter of children in the distance. I closed my eyes and focused on the gentle laps kissing the sand, instilled with a peace unlike anything I've ever felt before, as though drifting on a dream. The unveiling of the summer season resounded robustly!

My reverie was interrupted by the sound of familiar voices approaching. A little late but I didn't mind – it had given me a moment to appreciate my wonderful surrounds, which I admit to often neglecting. Louie plonked a plump bag of treats on the rug; it kept us going till the early evening. I'd offered to bring drinks as long as Louie brought his treats. He laid out the delectable spread and assured me he'd brought my favourite. We all agree that his pastizzi is the best in the land – I can't get enough of the ricotta and spinach – he says the secret lies in the fluffiness of the ricotta. Joe didn't hold back, lunging straight in and grabbing an imqaret.[2] We followed his lead, unable to resist the still-warm, freshly made pastries. We were silenced by our full mouthfuls until Helena spoke – she'd seemed in a pensive mood

---

[2] Date pastry

all day. She voiced some concerns about the war in Europe and asked if I knew any more about it. I knew a little more than most but certainly was not privy to the intelligence of the Maltese Command. Father hardly speaks to mother and I about the war, but you can certainly read him and he's been quite despondent of late. Judging by his demeanour and long silent pauses, concern weighs heavily on his mind. He's never been good at pretending that everything's fine when it's not. I do know he's apprehensive about the unpredictable whims of Mussolini. Perhaps that explains his recent disposition? Not wanting to create unnecessary worry via hearsay and assumption – because she has an anxiety-prone personality – I told Helena I wasn't sure, that I didn't know any more than she did. Before she could ask another question, Maria interrupted and changed the subject: 'Do you know what you're going to do?' Pointing to Joe and I. I looked at Joe who was staring out into the horizon in deep thought. For me, a daunting question; on the doorstep of adulthood, I didn't want to consider it, content on staying seventeen forever. But I had to confront the inevitable … I'm envious, but happy for them; the others seemingly have their lives sorted already. Helena and Louie are on their own paths, which align beautifully with their passions and talents; and of course Maria also has a set plan for her life. She aspires to marry a charming rich Frenchman and live out the rest of her days on the French Riviera; she's determined to make it happen, so much so she's promised to invite us all to her villa by the sea for a vacation, paying all our travel expenses! I'm certainly going to hold her to that one! As for Joe and I, we're not sure. Affectionately called 'the dreamers' by the others; in their words, 'we're still dreaming about the possibilities'. Joe and I are very alike, I think that's why we've been close friends since we were toddlers. We both have jobs, but it's not what we want for the long term. I love to write – I'm in my safe place when I allow my heart and mind to make its mark on the page. Words have the power to heal and change hearts – I've always been drawn to the innate strength of the written word. But I'm not sure how that translates to a meaningful career. As for Joe, we all know he's purposed for something greater, more significant, that aligns with his concern for others. I look up to him; I've never known anyone with such compassion, always there for anyone who needs help, to the point of giving the shirt off his back if need be. I've told him many times, I can see him living his life for the greater cause of other people. He always smiles bashfully and remains silent. It wouldn't surprise me one bit if he changed the world around him for the better – it's etched in his destiny.

I shrugged my shoulders and said, 'still don't know yet'. We all turned to Joe, still looking thoughtfully into the horizon. I love how half his mouth smiles when he ponders, forming a slight dimple in his cheek, I can't help but sigh affectionately at the sight. We got his attention. 'Joe … what are you going to do?' Causally, he said he's taking it one day at a time, that tomorrow is never guaranteed. His thoughtful response silenced us. We all turned our gaze towards the setting sun, mesmerised by the orange-red hues dancing on the ripples of the sea. As I was admiring nature's beautiful art, however, a sense of anxiety fell over me. A feeling of dread that somehow this summer will be different. At the time I thought it might have been because this was our last summer before becoming adults. Writing now, I don't think that was it – the sense was too unsettling. We headed home shortly after the sun set. I didn't say much as we packed and parted ways, consumed by my own reflections. Now that I think on it, the others seemed in a reflective mood also – perhaps something weighed on their minds too … I wonder if they sensed the same feeling I did.

RS

Narrative: up to June 1940

Malta was a bystander at this point of the Second World War and remained in a position of relative safety, surrounded by Allied French territory and bases in southern France, Corsica, Algeria and Tunisia. However, Malta was the only British base in the heart of the Mediterranean. The closest British bases were on the fringes of the Mediterranean: Alexandria in Egypt, 1,515 kilometres away, and Gibraltar, 1,780 kilometres away. The island was an ideal military base for any warring faction to use to gain the upper hand in the region: well positioned in the Mediterranean, mainland Europe to the north and Africa to the south, both in close proximity, and a clear eastward sea journey to the Middle East. It had a well-equipped natural harbour, ideal for a large naval fleet: a major land prong in the middle of the harbour surrounded by several smaller prongs, providing ample space for docking and repairs. The harbour, either side of the main prong, was over two kilometres long, meaning that the largest ships in the world could dock within its protective fortifications. Several imposing forts and high reinforced walls – built in the sixteenth century – at strategic points around the harbour provided extra cover and protection. The cliffs of the western coast stood over 100 metres tall; shallow rocky shores surrounded the coastline. Thus was Malta's coastline near impenetrable to sea invasion. The most effective form of invasion would be by air, to land aircraft or by paratroopers. The island's natural and well-built fortifications had protected them well throughout history. However, with the development of air power technology in the modern age, it was far from clear if the island could withstand an attack by air.

The year prior, Britain had concluded that Malta was not a safe harbour for Britain's Mediterranean naval fleet, citing the island as indefensible due to the growing power of the Italian air fleet. As a precaution, they relocated their Mediterranean fleet to Alexandria. In April 1940, the British Mediterranean Headquarters on the island was also moved to Alexandria. Such moves left Malta susceptible to an easy invasion; however, several submarines and torpedo boats remained, as well as a number of British defence force personnel and anti-aircraft guns stationed around the island's coast to assist in the event of an attack.

In late May, the French Prime Minister met with Churchill in London. They discussed the German incursion into northern France and the imminent invasion of southern France by the Italians amassing at the border. The French Prime Minister suggested giving the Italians land concessions in the hope of keeping them at bay and deterring them from officially joining the war. Malta was suggested as one such concession. However, the British War Cabinet was divided over the French Prime Minister's suggestion. Churchill was loathe to give in so easily as this would show weakness on Britain's part; he also understood the significance of holding on to Malta. He had to consider the situation carefully so as not to upset the Cabinet and jeopardise his standing amongst his peers, having only recently been appointed Prime Minister. After two days of deliberation, and during the continuing successful evacuation of the stranded troops at Dunkirk, Churchill was able to convince the Cabinet to fight on and not permit any concessions. Malta would not be surrendered without a fight.

At the beginning of June 1940, German forces rapidly gained ground southward into France from Belgium. The German tactic was relentless speed, a form of attack for which the Allies were unprepared – and unable to keep up with. They dominated with humiliating ease and by 5 June, German troops reached Amiens, 140 kilometres north of Paris. By 9 June, they reached Reims, 140 kilometres east of Paris. Paris was now surrounded and in their sights.

THE DECLARATION

Journal entry: 10 June 1940

Standing in the square as the crowd gathered to hear Mussolini speak – I'm certain this will be one of the few events in my life that is etched completely in my memory banks. Those moments you can vividly recall exactly where you were and what you felt, the sounds, the faces, the atmosphere. It seemed everyone from Valletta and the surrounding towns was present. The tension was dense; I could feel the weight resonating from the awaiting crowd as I weaved my way to a better position. I heard brief snippets of people's opinions on why Mussolini would or wouldn't join the war. The anxious babble continued until the megaphone atop the post office screeched. A chorus of 'shhh' swept through the crowd. Mario, the post office clerk positioned the radio so that Mussolini's speech could be amplified to the crowd. It's a good thing he's fluent in Italian, to translate for the majority who don't understand the language. There was absolute silence as Mussolini spoke. He spoke calmly at first, with great pauses in between sentences, which worked well for Mario's translating. Then, a few sentences into his speech, a collective gasping groan erupted from the crowd. Mussolini had declared war with Great Britain and France! The muffled cheer of the Italian crowd could be heard, chanting 'War! War!' I thought to myself, 'why would anyone celebrate war?!' As the speech continued, Mussolini's fervour increased, intensifying my concern and, by the looks of the surrounding faces, those of the crowd. Mussolini shouted his last words and the fanatical Italian crowd voiced their loudest cheer. It sent a disconcerting shiver right through me. Mussolini's speech was ominous, he was bent on power and the Italian crowd sounded ready to follow him into the abyss. Why? Why were they so happy about going to war? No one was attacking them or doing them any harm. The unnerving speech stilled the crowd to a stunned silence, dread manifesting on many faces. Children didn't understand what was going on but clung to their parents, sensing their fear. Parents reassured them unconvincingly. The panicked chatter increased amongst the crowd and I slithered my way through further. The evening sun pierced through a gap between buildings, hitting my eyes; a thought entered my mind: 'what would the setting sun be like tomorrow?' I caught sight of Joe in the distance; I approached him and we embraced. We don't usually hug when we see each other; I guess it was a spontaneous reaction to the uneasy situation. He asked if I was okay. Typical Joe, concerned for others! I wanted him to come with me to Lascaris, but he couldn't, he'd already organised with some other men to set up defensive positions at the Fort. His dedication to protecting others made me smile, despite the unsettling moment. It's comforting to know there are people like Joe in this world, who are determined to make it a better and safer place for everyone. We instinctively embraced once more before we parted ways, holding each other's gaze before the crowd obstructed our views of each other.

I'd never seen father so stressed. I stood against the wall at Lascaris watching the chaos unfold; I didn't want to get in any one's way. Commanders were strategising, notes passed around, telephones constantly ringing. I didn't realise it at the time but I was nibbling my fingernails for the first time ever. When father saw me, he did a double take. When he had a moment, he hastened to me, said to tell mother he'd be there for the night but would be home in the early hours to pick me up. I wanted to ask what was happening but I couldn't get a word in – he was immediately called away. I knew nothing for certain but if I had to make a guess … the alarming scene at Lascaris suggested an imminent threat.

On my way home, my thoughts had run wild. Would the Italians attack Malta? Surely not … But if they did, how could we match the might of such a powerful Goliath? Mussolini called out Britain and France, but didn't explicitly seek to contend with Malta. Then again, Malta is a British military base, so does that make us a target? The Maltese and Italians have been amicable over the centuries; indeed, there are many Italians on the island. Perhaps Mussolini's desire to recreate the Italian Kingdom has become a gluttonous ambition in addition to his fierce ego, incensed in recent times by Malta's quest to dissociate itself from the overarching shadow of Italian influence. I'm overwhelmed by the unprecedented anxiety. It's hard to imagine what this war would mean for my people, my loved ones and my country. Yesterday I was living free and without a care; today I feel drenched with fear, constricted by an unknown future. A precarious situation has fallen on our nation, subject to the whim of an erratic dictator. For the past year, the war was just a murmur in the wind, so far away from our land and minds. Now it may well arrive on Malta's doorstep! The storm clouds are gathering in the north and the threatening shadow builds in the distance; will it extend towards our land? I want to believe our shores will be spared but I can feel a gnawing feeling within begin to dominate, signalling a dire need to prepare for the worst. Fragments of Mussolini's determined speech echo in my mind, feeding my inner dread.

RS

Narrative: June 1940

Italian fascist leader and dictator, Benito Mussolini, had yet to declare his intentions regarding Italy's involvement in the war. In the preceding months, Germany and Great Britain had pressed Mussolini to take a side or to at least remain neutral. He withheld making a commitment until he was convinced of the direction in which the war was heading. When he saw how Germany was succeeding in asserting its dominance, gaining territorial ground with great ease, particularly in France – one of the key Allied powers – he wanted a piece of the glory.

On 10 June, city and town squares throughout Italy were filled to capacity, crowds waiting to hear Mussolini's speech broadcast via loud speakers. He was in Rome and would address the crowd from the second-storey balcony of Palazzo Venezia, overlooking the square. Enormous fascist symbols, adopted by Mussolini, adorned the columns on either side of the balcony – a bundle of sticks and an axe tied together – an ancient Imperial Roman symbol representing power. The fanatical devotees held up flags and banners of support for Mussolini. They chant 'Duce' (from the Latin, *dux*, meaning 'chief' or 'boss'). At 6:00 pm, he appeared on the balcony, rousing a mighty roar. He took a moment to behold the massive crowd, feeding off their energy. He signalled to the crowd to quiet down. In a posture of self-confidence, he took hold of his belt with both hands, around his lower abdomen, with head held high, asserting his masculinity. In just over a minute into his speech, he made his intentions crystal clear. Boisterous approval rumbled in response to his declaration of war; it took more than thirty seconds for the elation to dissipate. Mussolini called out Great Britain and France, which appeased the howling crowd further. He postulated that the hardships endured by the Italian people were due to the wealthy ruling class of the democratic West. He paused regularly, allowing the crowd to express their praise and support. He implied that Italy had done all it could to avoid a confrontation – but it now has no choice. He praised Germany and in particular Hitler, drawing a protracted cheer from the crowd. Nearing the end of his speech, he declared to the crowd that Italy would be victorious; banners lifted and flags waved passionately in rapturous applause and adulation. He ended with a call to arms: 'People of Italy!

Rush to arms and show your tenacity, your courage, your valour!'[3] The crowd once again lifted their voices in raucous support.

Mussolini's declaration of war against Great Britain and France meant that an attack on Malta was imminent. His allegiance with Hitler immediately increased the strategic value of the island; it was now a much-desired piece of land in the European–Mediterranean war arena. Whoever controlled Malta would hold dominance in the Mediterranean region, having access to safer shipping lanes, superior communications, and unconstrained military and civilian supplies between Europe and North Africa. For the British, the island was a pitstop for ships en route to the Suez Canal; a thoroughfare to India, Asia and Australia; and provided unhindered access to the Middle Eastern oil fields: the one thing most needed by each side to fuel their war campaign. To date, the British had enjoyed unchallenged control of the Mediterranean. However, Italy's involvement challenged their free movement in the region and, considering Italy's comparable military might, posed a major threat to British dominance. If Malta was lost to the Axis powers, this would most likely lead to the Middle East and North Africa being wrestled from Allied control. In turn, this would pave the way for a possible link with the Japanese empire, enlarging the Axis territory and military force – a catastrophic scenario for the free world.

Elsewhere in Europe, the Norwegians were unable to repel the German advance and surrendered. Germany continued their march southward towards Paris; French government officials fled from the capital and settled over 350 kilometres south in Vichy. The President of the USA, Franklin D. Roosevelt, maintained a stance of neutrality even after Mussolini's declaration; however, he pledged material support to the Allies in their fight against the Axis powers.

---

[3] Benito Mussolini's speech on 10 June 1940:
https://historicalresources.wordpress.com/2008/09/19/mussolini-speech-of-the-10-june-1940-declaration-of-war-on-france-and-england/

FIRST STRIKE

Journal entry: 11 June 1940

This morning, jolted awake by the sudden clanging of bells. In a sleepy daze, I wondered why I had set my alarm for 3 am. Then I remembered. In the first few moments of blissful ignorance, I had forgotten the looming danger. I sat up in a panic then remained still. Silence, except for the muffled conversation between father and mother in the kitchen. I'm surprised I slept so soundly, considering the anxiety of yesterday. I didn't want to leave father waiting so I got ready quickly and quietly, trying to hear their conversation. Father confirmed the anxious dread I had carried since yesterday evening. He told mother, 'they will attack today'. Stunned to a standstill by the gravity of this, my heart sank and the air rushed out of me. However, I soon shook myself out of my stupor; there was no time to dwell on my feelings. Mother voiced her concern for us, that we'd be in the middle of an attack. Father reassured her we'd be the safest people on the island at Lascaris, inadvertently reassuring me too. I was terrified of venturing into the epicentre of a bombardment, but I was eager to be of service – I felt a strong call to duty to my country and my people. But I was torn though; although I left with father, I didn't want to leave mother alone. Father kept reminding her to seek underground shelter beneath the Basilica as soon as the air raid siren sounded. I took comfort knowing she'd be safe should there be any danger. Mother nodded nervously to his warning. 'Please be safe', she repeated while fiddling anxiously with her crucifix pendant. She stood at the doorway and didn't take her eyes off us until we drove out of sight.

I've walked through the tunnels that lead to Lascaris many times before, but today the atmosphere was unnerving. The echoes of our footsteps and the periodic drips of water into puddles gave me shivers. Lascaris was the most lively I've ever seen it. I was so overwhelmed I didn't know what to do. Father immediately joined the officers convened around the large map table in the centre of the room; with long sticks they pushed around pawn-like-figures as they strategised. The chalkboards, which were usually bare, were now bursting with information. There were women on the mezzanine managing the telephones, going to and fro, passing on information. I took a deep breath and did what I usually do – went to my small desk and began to organise paperwork – unprecedented piles of it!

The land remained still in the hours before dawn, but the chaotic activity at Lascaris increased as we drifted closer to first light. A frenzied chatter filled the background air, and shouted information and instructions sounded above all other noise. I don't think anyone knew exactly what was about to happen, but there was a collective sense that something would happen soon. I kept looking at the clock, willing for more seconds to pass without an attack arriving. Then at 6:55 am, I was arrested by the loudest shout in the room all morning. It sent a bone-chilling shudder through me. 'Sound the sirens, sound the sirens!' I wouldn't have thought it possible but the room became even more chaotic; everyone scrambling except me. I stood still in disbelief, clutching a pile of papers close to my chest. I struggled to breathe, a pool of distress blurred my vision; I looked upward, my thoughts turned to the people above ground and what they would endure. I felt completely helpless about the dire situation about to envelop my family and friends, my people and my country. I attempted to pray, which I hadn't done since I was confirmed. I wished mother were with me; she knows how to pray properly. I'm not certain what I believe, but I wished I had her faith in that moment. Suddenly, the chatter wound to a deafening silence, as though someone abruptly turned down a radio's volume dial. The hush endured except for the whispers of some imperative communications. The whole roomful of people tried to anticipate the moment of the first strike. A distant thunderous thud, then another, and another – it kept coming. A tsunami of metal rain swept over the land. Earth-shaking tremors followed each thud; in unison, we flinched in fear as bombs landed metres above.

After the first sirens sounded, the thunderous thuds stopped, and the faint buzz of aircraft faded. I was relieved, thinking the worst was over. How wrong I was! It wasn't long before the siren sounded again and another aerial assault began, and it continued to rain throughout the day. By nightfall, I had lived through the longest day of my life. But with the night came peace; the sirens, the aircraft danger, and the falling sky finally ceased. Father was ordered to go home and get some proper rest; he hadn't been home in three days.

Not one to sugar-coat reality, father asserted that tomorrow would be much the same. We emerged from the tunnel and took a moment to assess the damage – as much as could be seen in the darkness. The streets were empty, apart from those preparing to leave. We walked past two large craters in the ground, destroyed buildings, rubble spilled onto the streets. Smoke rose all around and lingered in the air, people scurrying, carrying plump bags. Father said it's best they move away from the city, they'll be safer. I overheard a mother say to her children, they'd be staying in Zebbug with Nanna and Nannu for a while. Already saddened by the sudden destruction of our beautiful capital, I was pained to know there would be more to come. Father and I didn't talk much on our way home. At one point, I faced him to ask a question about the war, but then didn't. I could see the anguish and fatigue on his face, so instead, I asked how he was doing. He took some moments to respond. He said he was okay, but concerned about how to best protect our people. I don't blame him – I suspect such a significant responsibility would break me. I'm not going to ask father about the war. I'll leave it up to him to tell me what he wants to. I feel that asking will only add to his already burdened shoulders. Now that I think about it, I've never known mother to ask him about his days at Lascaris either.

When we turned into our street, I fixed my eyes intently on my home as soon as it came into view, hoping to see mother. And there she was, waiting for us at the front door, visibly relieved the moment she saw us pull up; with hands clasped, she mouthed a prayer of gratitude. I impulsively ran to her. We all stood there on the front porch and embraced for a while. The first day of Malta forcibly entering the war had rattled us – we'd never embraced like that before.

As I write these closing words on this day, 11 June 1940, I can truly say that it has been the worst day of my short life. Yet, there's a disturbing sense in the pit of my stomach that worse days are to come. This morning, when I first heard we were going to be attacked, it felt surreal, so hard to believe. After the day's events, though, it has hit home. This is now my real life. Malta is being bombed, the war has infected our land. My life and the lives of all Maltese people have changed from this day forth. I felt a piece of my youthful innocence chipped away today by the hammer blow of brutish wickedness. A week ago, I was at the beach enjoying the first days of summer. Today began the demise of that pleasant summer sunrise, the chirping morning birds, and the floral fragrance upon the relieving breeze. Replaced by dark plumes obstructing the sun's shine, the whistle of bombs overhead, and the aroma of destruction.

RS

Narrative: June 1940

In a little over twelve hours since its declaration, Italy's first act of involvement in the Second World War was an attack on Malta. On 11 June 1940, at approximately 6:55 am, warning sirens wailed throughout the country. The Italian Air Force, Regia Aeronautica, launched from an air base in Sicily and conducted their first aerial attack. At the time, Malta was not equipped or prepared for the outbreak of war. There were less than fifteen anti-aircraft guns scattered around the island, one main operational airfield, and the only fighter planes on the island were obsolete Gloster Gladiator biplanes. From the outset, it seemed inevitable that Malta would rapidly crumble before the military giant.

The Gloster Gladiator biplanes had been found in large packing crates some months earlier, left by a British aircraft carrier. Biplanes were predominantly used in the First World War and had become obsolete by the 1940s. Compared to modern fighter aircraft, the biplanes were much slower, reaching a top speed of only 250 kilometres per hour, and possessed limited technology; they were certainly no match for the modern Italian aircraft that could double their speed. The one advantage of the biplanes was their smaller size, which made them easily manoeuvrable. Six Gloster Gladiator biplanes were available to be assembled; however, due to a lack of spare parts, only three could be committed to Malta's air defence. The Gladiators were given the names *Faith*, *Charity* and *Hope*.

At the end of the first day, the Regia Aeronautica had reached Malta several times, which included three bombing raids, two major attacks at sunrise, one before sunset, and three reconnaissance flyovers. The fighters piloting the Gladiators, coupled with the anti-aircraft gunners on the ground, did well to partially deter the attack but were overwhelmed by the sheer number of Italian aircraft. Bombs were dropped on Valletta and the surrounding cities, the Grand Harbour, the dockyards and the airfield. Italy's attack created a mass exodus. Within a few days of the first strike, approximately 100,000 people had left Valletta and the surrounding harbour area, fleeing to safer inland areas.

For the next ten days, the three Gladiators provided Malta's only aerial defence until the island's air fleet was bolstered by the British. Although the Gladiators struggled to keep up with the Regia Aeronautica, they provided minimum aerial defence and, more importantly, played a significant role in boosting the morale of the people – indicating that the nation could indeed put up a fight against its aggressors. The Gladiators continued to take the skies in the following months; however, their service would ultimately come to an end. *Charity* was shot down in July 1940; *Hope* was destroyed in an air raid in February 1941; and *Faith* survived the war, albeit in a dilapidated state. The RAF restored the aircraft and presented it to the people of Malta in September 1943.

On mainland Europe, the French gave up their resistance against the Germans, effectively surrendering. In an attempt to protect Paris from destruction, the French Government declared Paris an open city, allowing the German troops to enter Paris unopposed.

3. The Gloster Gladiator biplane 'Faith' restored on display at the Malta War Museum, Valletta. Presented to the Maltese people by the Royal Air Force.

WAR ROOM SORROW

Journal entry: 13 June 1940

Tonight, I write the most painful words I've ever written. Yet I know any words will fail to convey my anguish and gripping devastation. Constant streams of sorrow have poured down my face since I was told the news. As I sit here, trembling, inscribing my deepest sadness, tears fall fittingly onto the page, a lasting stain to mark this day's incomparable grief. A life-defining moment, etched in my eternal memory; the when, where, and intense emotions of this day will never be forgotten …

It was early afternoon. I took a break at my desk to eat a tomato paste and olive oil sandwich mother had made. I was watching the commanders strategising on the floor when I noticed a low-ranking officer rush into the room and hand a note to father. His disposition changed as he read; whatever was on that note troubled him deeply. Abruptly, he looked over at me. In that instant, I was struck with a sense of dread. I instinctively gulped down the mouthful I was chewing on and placed the rest of the sandwich on the table. I knew there and then – whatever was on that note was connected to me. He looked back down at the note in dismay, then with his head still downward, made his way towards me. He held that note tightly with both hands, not making eye contact until we were face to face. I lifted myself up; weakened by an increasing sense of anxiety, my heartbeat soared, throat tightened and jaw clenched, instinctively preparing for the worst. Without saying a word, his look all but told me the truth. He opened his mouth to speak but struggled to form the words. It's so unlike him to dither, which only added to the frenzy of emotions inside me. A slow pool of tears welled in my eyes and I impatiently blurted, 'is it mother?' Hastily, he assured me she was fine. My immediate sense of relief was countered by growing confusion. He explained that during Malta's first attack, six volunteers were guarding the tip of Valletta; explosives fell in the vicinity and all perished. He paused. Of course, I was deflated by the news and looked at him in bewilderment. He continued: among them was a teenage boy. In that moment, I felt terror rise and my breaths become deeper; once again my eyes pooled in fear. There was one person I knew who would have risked their life for others that way. Through blurry eyes and quivering lips, I faintly asked, 'Joe?' He nodded ever so slightly. I broke. My eyes released a deluge and a gust of breath left me, bringing me to my knees, utterly sapped. Father did his best to comfort me. He wanted to take me home but I wanted to stay. I felt an inexplicable comfort being there, in close proximity to the place where Joe took his last breaths. Father took me to a private room to grieve alone, and grieve I did.

On our journey home, although nothing was said, I could feel father grieving with me. Joe was like a son to him, having known him since he was a little boy; mother was just as distraught over the news. In this shattered state of being, nothing else seems to matter now; the sheer ruthlessness of this war has dispelled my fear utterly. I don't know if that feeling will last but I know I'm changed forever. I've been broken by the reality and tragedy of life, as though I'm seeing this wicked and warped world for the first time – for what it truly is. However, I must remember that sprinkles of goodness exist, people like Joe, and for his sake, I want to carry on his legacy, to make a profound difference to my people and my country.

Dearest Joe, my eternal hero. The first time we met was on our very first day of school. At lunch, you were sitting across from me when a stray ball knocked my lunch from my hands. You saw me in tears, and you came over and shared your lunch with me. Your heart was on display from the moment we met – inseparable ever since. Oh Joe, I'm wallowing in the stricken depths and I don't know if I can ever come out this place. Life with you there is all I've ever known. I try to compose myself by thinking about what you would say if you were here; the echoes of your inspiration and perseverance relieve the uncertainty within a little. The world is a much lesser place without you, the bright light of a rare soul extinguished by an ever-darkening world.

My restless heart won't let me sleep. I've spent the last few hours clutching a photo of us from the Sliema Fiesta last summer. I don't think I've ever had that much fun. I think back through our years of both lighthearted joviality and deep heart-to-hearts. Secrets shared, sworn between us and no one else. Your calm, cheerful outlook on life always made me happier and put me at peace. I've never felt more at ease than when I was with you.

Joe, now that you're gone, I must confess a repressed notion of us that I hid in my heart. A feeling I had withheld because I was unsure of what it meant. I was afraid of the outcome if you didn't relate to it, share it. I wish I had brought it up with you; you would have made sense of it and, of course, with your selfless nature, you would have dealt with the matter with nothing but gentleness and respect. I had told you everything in my life except for this one thing; now I've lost that chance, forever, to tell you how I truly felt. My heart will never fully recover because a piece of my heart remains lost with you. Your absence leaves a permanent scar in my life that will always be with me.

It's not fair Joe! Why did you have to go? The one person who could comfort me in this moment is the one I'm grieving. I take some small solace thinking back to the last time we saw each other. Coincidentally bumping into you in the square. I recall how we instinctively embraced. Now, thinking back on that moment, I can't help but imagine that divine hands made us cross paths one last time so I would always have that moment with you – a rare embrace I will cherish for the rest of my life. Next week we would have celebrated your eighteenth birthday. You may not have reached adulthood in this life, but you perished a man. Goodbye, my sweet friend, my soulmate, my kindred spirit. I will carry you with me from this day forth: your immense heart to inspire me, your words to encourage me, and your soul to comfort me. You will never be forgotten.

RS

Narrative: June 1940

On the first day of the Italian attack, explosives fell on the tip of Upper Fort St. Elmo in Valletta, one kilometre from the Lascaris War Rooms. At approximately 7:45 am, military and civilian personnel were guarding the Fort from a possible land invasion by Italian paratroopers. Five men and a teenage boy were killed by the blast – the first casualties of the war on Malta.

The Lascaris War Rooms were used to conduct military affairs; all war operations involving Malta and the Mediterranean, whether land, air or sea, were conducted from within. Lascaris was equipped with everything needed to conduct military operations, as well as suitable living quarters with supplies and bunks. The main gallery contained a mezzanine level for those working telecommunications, overlooking a large table map of Sicily. Connecting to the War Rooms was an underground complex of tunnels and chambers that weaved beneath Valletta. The rooms and tunnels had existed for centuries and were built by the Knights of St. John in the 16th century for their military campaigns. The vast underground network inadvertently provided a ready-made protective headquarters for the Maltese Command and the British to conduct their war efforts, while also providing shelter for the Maltese people during bombardment. The War Rooms were enlarged to house the almost 1,000 personnel that would operate daily in the rooms and tunnels throughout the war. The Maltese Command had existed since before the war and operated independently from the British Army. They had been responsible for defending Malta for decades. However, their involvement in the war would require further military power and personnel. Thus, they worked closely with the British military to defend the nation and its people.

Underground shelters continued to be built throughout the war, not only in Valletta but in other highly populated areas. Many underground tunnels and shelters existed throughout the island from centuries past, including catacombs and modern disused railway tunnels; however, more shelters were required to house the majority of the population. The ancient tunnels were built at a time when the population of Malta was less than 50,000. The lack of heavy drilling machinery meant that digging had to be done by hand; the military and thousands of volunteers used what was available to them, the most basic of hand tools, hammers and pick axes, buckets on strings, and horses with carts. Fortunately, conditions were favourable; the whole island rested upon soft limestone rock, which meant it could be dug out easily, even by hand. For many, the shelters would become a permanent home during bombardments. By mid-1942, an additional twenty kilometres of underground tunnel space was built to keep the Maltese people safe.

On mainland Europe, on 14 June, German troops triumphantly marched into Paris after its declaration as an open city. The invasion of France was a massive disaster; almost 100,000 soldiers lost their lives and over 1.7 million were taken as prisoners. As German troops continued southward, so did civilians, creating an exodus of millions fleeing the tyranny of German occupation. On 16 June, Paul Reynaud resigned as French Prime Minister and was replaced by Marshal Petain, a hero of the First World War. His immediate directive was to seek an armistice with Germany. An armistice was agreed to on 22 June. Two days later, the French also agreed to terms with the Italians who were advancing in the south-east. The armistice with Germany meant that Petain held office in the city of Vichy, in the centre of France. France was now split into two – occupied and unoccupied zones – and movement between the zones was prohibited. The Nazi regime gave Petain limited autonomy to oversee most of southern France, autonomy that remained at the whim of Nazi command. The Germans could have swept up the rest of France with ease, but Hitler allowed a French puppet government to nominally rule southern France to give the impression that France had allied itself with the Axis powers. This was a demoralising psychological blow to the British, who now had to battle the Axis juggernaut on their own. The domination of France meant that the Nazis also had influence over the French North African territories of Algeria and Tunisia. Hitler was delighted by the French surrender and celebrated by taking a victory tour of Paris. He sought retribution after Germany's demoralising defeat during the First World War. He insisted the French Armistice be signed in the same railway carriage in which Germany's armistice agreement was signed in 1918. Once the formalities were over, Hitler ordered the carriage to be sent to Berlin for public display.

By 25 June, the Nazi war machine had swept through Europe. Hitler held supremacy of most of Europe, excluding those countries that had declared neutrality: Sweden, Portugal, Ireland, Iceland, Spain, Switzerland, Andorra, Monaco, Liechtenstein, Vatican City, San Marino and Turkey. Axis territory had expanded north and south of Malta. To the north, the Axis-held southern European coastline stretched from the borders of Spain to Greece. To the south, the Axis North African coastline stretched from Morocco to Egypt. Thus, Malta was surrounded and perilously vulnerable. The nearest British bases were Gibraltar and Alexandria, both over 1,500 kilometres away; whereas the Axis bases of Sicily and Tripoli were only 100 and 350 kilometres away, respectively.

Now that mainland Europe was subdued, the Axis war efforts shifted to Great Britain. The Nazi occupation of France meant that they were now located just over the English Channel, only some forty kilometres wide at the narrowest point. The Axis powers successfully annexed part of British territory; by 1 July, the Germans had invaded the Channel Islands, Guernsey and Jersey. During the next few months, the RAF would engage with the Luftwaffe in the 'Battle of Britain'. The Germans launched a blitz campaign over Britain, continual waves of aerial bombardment targeting London and industrial cities and infrastructure. However, after months of battle, the Luftwaffe failed to gain air superiority over Britain and, by October, officially abandoned the Battle, reverting to periodic bombing raids until May 1941.

4. Memorial dedicated to the first casualties of the war on Malta on Fort St. Elmo. The inscription: 'These six men were the first soldiers to die in Malta in the Second World War'; 'Killed in action on this very spot at 7:45 am 11 June 1940'.

5. Lascaris War Rooms: main control room. Preserved as a museum in Valletta.

RELIEF

Journal entry: 2 August 1940

The howl in the air and the thuds on the land are incessant: the new anthem of the nation. My ears have adapted to the sound; even when the bombings fall silent, an echo remains throughout the night like the sporadic strike of a timpani drum. A haunting fatigue has seized me and continuous sleep has become an elusive commodity. Gone are the days I sleep past dawn. These days I wearily wake well before shards of light pierce the sky. With sadness, I've realised that in all my life till now, I've never taken the time to witness the rising sun.

However, the exhaustion of my physical being is of lesser concern than the emotional and psychological bombardment of my mind. I know that if I surrender my mind, every part of me will succumb with it. Conflict rages within every day, as I wrestle for control of my will. I've set the goal to be victorious one day at a time; with each successful new day, I feel a sense of renewal while learning to cohabit with the enemy of my despondent thoughts. Becoming accustomed to the struggle, I manage to overwhelm the dogged feelings of capitulation by recalling the core purpose and inspiration regarding why I must keep going – it's not just about me, it's about my family, my friends, my people. Their homes and livelihoods are gradually diminishing, the lack of basic necessities dwindling by the day. The heart-rending heartache of loved ones lost, but impending dangers do not allow time to properly grieve. I know this feeling too well. I think about Joe every day, but suffer a want of closure, not having had an appropriate farewell.

When I am at Lascaris, I am consumed by the dire situation, my thoughts meandering into despairing contemplation while I file. The situation on the ground is ominous; we are progressively crushed by the Axis bombs. Our resistance in the air is near non-existent. Attempts to improve our situation seem like wishes on dandelion dust that disappear quickly in the wind. Another day, another step closer in the downward spiral inevitably ending in defeat – I am resigned to the worst.

But, today, there was suddenly a uniform cheer and subsequent rapturous applause. A delivery of air reinforcements had safely arrived! A fleet of aircraft that will take to the skies over Malta to challenge the enemy. What a relief it was amidst the constraining despair, the news like warm water running through me, loosening the grip of strangling unease. It was a godsend at just the right time. Mother described the jubilation of the townspeople when they saw the British reinforcements grace the skies above, like angels sweeping in to guard the nation. It was a win of sorts, a small glimmer of motivation to keep the spirit afloat, and we needed it! A timely reminder that, despite the forbidding situation, the palpable struggle for longevity, the ache of a burdened heart, sudden uplifting moments are yet possible, the slightest relieving breath to spark an enduring hope.

RS

Narrative: June–August 1940

Air raid attacks on Malta had been consistent since 11 June; further, a new threat appeared from the south, waves of bombers launching from Italian bases in Libya. On 22 June, six Hawker Hurricane fighters would reach Malta as a much-needed boost to their air defence. The Hurricanes, although also somewhat dated, were far superior to the Gladiator biplanes; they were more durable and easily manoeuvrable, in addition to reaching speeds of up to 530 kilometres per hour.

However, Malta's air defence remained overwhelmingly outnumbered. By 19 July, only one working aircraft, a Gladiator, was left to defend Malta. This high attrition rate was inevitable due to the continuous bombardment; by the end of July, Malta would endure its one hundredth air raid.

In early August, the island's air fleet was bolstered again with four bombers and twelve Hurricanes. Such attempts to supply the enemy-surrounded island required extreme vigilance and subterfuge. The aircraft took off from aircraft carriers at a safe distance, some 500 kilometres away. Simultaneously, escorting sea vessels launched a surprise attack on the Italian Cagliari airfield in Sardinia. The attack was a success; Italian aircraft were destroyed and the replacement aircraft reached Malta safely. Along with the aircraft were additional airmen; there were now enough aircraft and pilots to form Malta's first fighter squadron.

The supply of aircraft to the isolated island was one hurdle, but the supply of military and civilian provisions was another; such supplies could only be brought in by sea, which had become a hazardous undertaking. The Italians were a constant presence in the western Mediterranean, active between the supply routes of Sicily and North Africa. Britain no longer had convoy protection from French naval ports and air bases in southern France, Algeria and Tunisia, which now lay passive under Axis command. The British Cabinet had deemed the sea between Gibraltar and Malta too perilous for sending supplies, which also affected the supply routes to Egypt and the Middle East. It was determined that all major convoys were to sail around the continent of Africa, a journey of over 20,000 kilometres. Malta had to wait up to three months to receive supplies from the time they were approved by the British Cabinet. Once the supplies reached Egypt, they were sent to Malta via the eastern Mediterranean, which was deemed a safer route due to Turkey and Greece's neutrality at that time.

Another battle of the air was waged via radio transmissions from mainland Italy. An attempt to attack the psychological wellbeing of the Maltese and diminish their morale. Spoken in the Maltese language, false propaganda reports espoused progress on the island and of the Axis powers throughout Europe. In one broadcast, the Italian service boasted about destroying Malta's railways; however, Malta's railways had not been in use the past nine years. Malta began a daily radio broadcast to counter the false claims being made by the Italian broadcast.

Elsewhere, the British were concerned about the French naval fleet in Mers El Kébir, near Oran, Algeria. The French surrender and armistice with Germany and Italy meant that the French warships moored in the Mediterranean could potentially pose a threat to the Allies. The British sent a delegate to Algeria to request control of the fleet or their relocation far from Axis reach. The French refused to negotiate, instead assuring the British that the French fleet would remain under French control. However, this did not quell British concerns, considering the rapid capitulation of France and Hitler's ease so far in seizing whatever he desired. Consequently, the British had no choice but to neutralise French ships docked at port. On 3 July, the Royal Navy attacked the French fleet at Mers El Kébir, destroying three battleships. While in Britain, several French battleships and destroyers – docked in British waters – were attained, and the French naval force in Alexandria was disarmed. Understandably, the relationship between France and Britain turned hostile, and Vichy France ceased diplomatic relations with Britain. The relationship between the two states remained frosty in the years to follow.

In late July, the USSR encroached on the border of Poland by consuming the Baltic states of Estonia, Latvia and Lithuania, increasing Stalin's footprint on the European mainland. In his quest for power, Hitler made secret plans to invade the USSR in the first half of the following year. Mussolini continued his attacks on weaker opposition; on 4 August, he invaded British-controlled Somaliland from Italian East Africa (Ethiopia), taking full control of the region by 17 August.

At this time, the British remained the only Allied power in the war. They bore the responsibility of keeping the Axis powers from progressing southward, defending the Mediterranean and North Africa while also defending their homeland. The only Allied combative assistance at that time were the inhabitants of the lands they controlled, such as Malta. As the war progressed, the British were losing aircraft and naval vessels at an alarming rate and were running out of funds to pay for the equipment needed to maintain their war efforts against the rapid pace of the Axis powers. Churchill proposed a plan to the United States President in the hopes of replenishing the British arsenal. On 13 August, Churchill and Roosevelt entered a lend-lease arrangement that would later be officially adopted by the United States Congress in March 1941. The arrangement meant that Britain would receive military equipment in exchange for 99-year leases of British territories to the USA, to be used as air and naval bases. The first exchange occurred in September. The USA supplied Britain with fifty destroyer warships for leases on bases in Newfoundland and the Caribbean. In this way, the Americans were able to aid their allies while still avoiding direct involvement in the war. Roosevelt was keen to assist Churchill; however, Congress and the American people wanted neutrality. Thus, the lend-lease arrangement allowed Roosevelt to assist the British while refraining from engaging American personnel.

ONE HUNDRED DAYS

Journal entry: 19 September 1940

It's been 100 days living under the shadow of intimidation. It might as well be 1,000 days; I would not be able to tell the difference. I can only vaguely recall what life was like before the conflict began; reminiscences of a previous life linger dimly in the dungeons of my mind, buried beneath the burdensome contemplations necessitated by the presence of war. Such recollections are further suppressed by the blaring sirens, the harassing buzz above and the hammer-blows on land, shoved ever deeper into the furthest recesses of my mind. But on the rare occasion, when all is still, if I close my eyes, concentrate, and dig through the mental bog, there, even if for a brief moment, I inhale the faint memory of a floral fragrance carried on a cool summer's breeze, I can hear the soothing sound of winter's tears running down my bedroom window as I am cosy in bed reading a book. Sadly, such recollections are rare – previously, I had rarely paused to absorb the small moments of life. How I wish I had cherished such moments with greater awareness!

It seems such a shame that an oppressive situation and sustained adversity were required for me to come to an appreciation of the simple beauty of everyday life. But the contamination of war has instilled a sensitivity in me to nature's wonder and a renewed gratefulness. Now for instance, as I've been writing, I've paused several times to gaze out my window, lured by the radiance of the full moon. I've never thought much on how it's always there, floating in space so close to the earth. Mirroring the sun's light to provide light for us to see with at night. Amazing! A sight to which I would not have given a second glance before the war. It's as though I'm seeing the full moon for the first time, lost in the strength of its grandeur.

With regret, I recall a missed moment of wonder amongst the daily gloom. Yesterday afternoon, as I made my way through the rubble-reduced abandoned streets of Valletta, I was so absorbed by the surrounding destruction that I wasn't interested to gaze upon a tiny out-of-place splash of vibrant yellow in my peripheral vision. It was the only colour in the stone-riddled, dust-covered landscape. But I allowed discouraging thoughts to consume me and ignored nature's tiny motivation. This morning, I realised what I had not recognised yesterday. The splash of colour was not just a lively cluster of Bermuda buttercups – more important, they thrived within a sea of stone debris and dust, covering every inch of ground; nevertheless, they poked through the lifeless terrain, and danced sweetly in the autumn breeze. I'm inspired by their tenacity, fragile life with the innate perseverance to stand resolute in imposing and brutish surrounds. I walked the same path this afternoon, wanting to admire them properly, but they were gone. Perhaps consumed by new rubble, perhaps someone appreciated them more than I did, plucked them from the ground and kept them as a symbol of hope. I promise now, I will no longer neglect to bathe in the splendour of these small yet significant glimpses of wonder that form nature's messages of inspiration. In the normal everyday, when all is well, such inspiration is easily overlooked and unappreciated. But such beauty is profoundly enhanced against the ugliness of destruction. I believe such sparks of beauty exist to bring hope to the dreary-laden heart. These precious morsels of inspiration have instilled some hope within me for a better tomorrow, if need be, to get me through another 100 days.

RS

Narrative: September 1940

The Axis had established their presence around Malta: Italy to the north, Tunisa to the east, Libya to the south. The eastern region was relatively clear; however, Egypt, Greece and Crete were under constant threat. Malta was growing more isolated and increasingly dependent on the outside world for help and crucial supplies. As time went on, military and civilian resources were becoming exhausted and supplies were desperately needed to rejuvenate the island. For the civilian population, food and medical supplies were of greatest need. The military required machine reinforcements, ammunition and spare plane parts; of most concern was the shortage of fuel. It was estimated that Malta could run out within two months. The loss of fuel would spell the end of Malta's offensive and defensive efforts and would leave the way open for invasion by Axis forces. Resupplying Malta was made all the more hazardous by the Italian deployment of sea mines around the island to impede merchant ships. At that time, Malta had only one minesweeping vessel to remove or destroy the tens of thousands of sea mines.

Regardless of these perils, an attempt had to be made to replenish Malta. A convoy operation was launched in early September. It would be the first large convoy made from Alexandria, carrying over 35,000 tons. The journey was not without interruption; Italian forces intercepted the convoy and inflicted minor damage, but it ultimately reached port safely. While the supplies were being unloaded, two air raid attacks attempted to destroy the vessels at dock. However, these attacks were unsuccessful and the much-needed military and civilian supplies were unloaded without further hindrance. The Admiral of the convoy was to return the fleet to Alexandria; however, he decided to also attack Italian airfields in Rhodes, 530 kilometres north of Alexandria. The surprise ambush was very effective; they were able to attack several Italian airfields before returning safely to Alexandria. The successful convoy operation was very timely and improved the island's situation.

In mid-September, Mussolini ordered an Italian force of 250,000 men, based in occupied Libya, to invade Egypt. He exploited the vulnerability of the British at a time when they were focused on protecting the motherland, under an intense German bombing campaign that month. The Italians reached 100 kilometres within Egypt's boarder and settled at Sidi Barrani. The Egyptian invasion required Italian air units to be redirected to North Africa, which meant that air attacks on Malta were greatly reduced for a time. This allowed Malta's forces to regroup and plan further offensive measures. The lack of bombardment also allowed supplies to reach Malta in relative safely. By late September, although some attacks occurred with minimal effects, a full cargo from Alexandria comprising almost 50,000 tons of anti-aircraft artillery and ammunition was delivered, replenishing the island's military capabilities and armoury even further and delivering over 1,000 personnel.

Elsewhere, the Austro-Hungarian Empire collapsed. This led to the formation of Romania, Hungary and Yugoslavia. Disagreement about land allotment between Hungary and Romania gestured towards conflict. Hitler did not want a regional war; he relied on Romanian oil and did not want an internal conflict to deplete those reserves he needed for his own war ambitions. Hitler sought to placate the situation, but neither party would be entirely satisfied. Ultimately, however, the contested land was divided between the two, avoiding further conflict.

On 27 September, Germany, Italy and Japan signed the Tripartite Pact, an Axis alliance that formed an economic, political and military superpower, pledging war on any nation that attacked an Axis nation. The aim of the pact was to prevent other nations joining the war in the European and Asian arena; it was specifically intended to deter the USA. Later, several Balkan states would also become signatories to the pact.

THE EMPIRE STRIKES BACK

Journal entry: 12 November 1940

Undulating joy met with an underlying sense of guilt. A raucous cheer resounded at Lascaris, and a part of me wanted to join the jubilant chorus. Instead, I watched the celebration with quieter contentment and relief. The British had annihilated the Italian naval base at Taranto. But the news sparked a conflict within me. There must have been great destruction and casualties, yet their despair and sadness equalled relief and delight for us. What I once thought were my sound judgements had reached a crossroads. The complexities of this war have come to challenge my moral standards. I certainly do not take delight in devastation, yet the result of such a preventative strike means a reprieve, limiting bombardment for a time and guaranteeing a safer passage for supplies, easing the struggles of my people. It's one thing to defend an attack, but to be the aggressor … well, this is where I wrestle with the absolutes of right and wrong. My naïve youthful ideas continue to be chipped away; gone is my perception of the inherent goodness of the human heart, gone is my belief that the world is primarily a good place. The reality of mankind reveals its foul stench. I heard a scripture once that has stayed with me from my youth. I didn't believe it but now see how apt it is, it even applied to me: 'The heart is deceitful above all things and beyond cure. Who can understand it?' The ethical labyrinth of wartime engagement has raised questions that beg for answers, to comfort my questioning mind.

But I think such answers are out of reach, perpetually dwelling in an indeterminate grey area.

The British offensive has lifted the spirits of the people, and with the improving situation on the ground in recent times, there's reason to be hopeful. The intensity of attacks has greatly eased. Although the remnants of war remain – the warning sirens, the curfews, the rations, the destruction – the people have adjusted remarkably well to our wartime reality. Faces gleam with gratitude eating a bland boiled potato. Families content to create minimalistic shelters underground. Children play in the streets with boundless laughter; their gleeful abandon seems to defy the fact of being in a war – they even utilise the rubble as part of their games! The people emboldened enough to leave the underground shelters during a raid, to watch and cheer the RAF as they repel the Regia Aeronautica.

I believe I have realised the most important aspect of the people's resolve. Yes, to maintain health and safety; the nourishment of the body is vital. But it's the nourishment of the minds, hearts and soul that creates an enduring spirit. The morale of the people is the nation's most crucial commodity – for its longevity. This was evident today as I saw the first Christmas displays. The people are determined not to let the surrounding devastation deter their joy in celebrating these most cherished festivities. I had been oblivious to the upcoming occasion, but the festive sights reminded me that Christmas is only six weeks away. There was a pleasant joviality in the air while houses were decorated: sparkling tinsel of red and green, strings of light bordering windows, nativity scenes in front of houses, and Christmas trees in the process of being ornately dressed. This is something I had witnessed many times before, but without sentiment. However, this time, it became an inspiring moment; seeing the people radiating their hope strengthened my own hope. Even surrounded by destruction and uncertainty about the future, they persist, giving me the sense that even if this war endures long, the people would endure longer.

RS

Narrative: October–November 1940

The British War Cabinet came to the consensus that to maintain regular and safe access throughout the Mediterranean, North Africa and the Middle East, Italy must be subdued and Malta must be strengthened; this acknowledged that maintaining the strategic island would be pivotal to Allied success in the region. The War Cabinet made haste during a lull in air attacks, sending personnel, supplies, artillery and tanks, including the very effective heavy and light anti-aircraft guns; these fortified the perimeter of the island, bringing the total of anti-aircraft guns to over 100.

The RAF had become the dominant power of the sky, which was embarrassing for the Italians. The Regia Aeronautica fleet outnumbered and outclassed the Malta-based aircraft; however, they were overwhelmed by the skill of the RAF pilots. In fact, in some instances, when Italian bombers saw the RAF approaching to meet them, they would return to base. In the first week of November, the British increased their offensive efforts against the Italians. A bombing raid was launched from Malta on mainland Italy, targeting Naples and Brindisi, striking the ports, industrial facilities and railway lines. A few days later, Malta received a large convoy from Alexandria and Gibraltar. Malta's air supremacy deterred Italian attacks and allowed for safer passage of supply convoys via the western Mediterranean, rather than going around the African continent. The threat of enemy attack was constantly present; however, the risk was mitigated by the reinforcement of Malta's offensive and defensive positions and the Allies' supremacy in the Mediterranean skies.

Following the arrival of supplies, the British planned another offensive strike on 11 November. The target was a southern Italian naval base at Taranto. It was an all-air attack, consisting of twenty-one torpedo bombers launched from the aircraft carrier HMS *Illustrious*. The aim was to destroy facilities and the battleship fleet. The attack was a success, causing significant damage while losing only two aircraft. Of the six battleships at port, two were damaged, and one was irreparable. The attack also damaged the dockyard and a sea aircraft base, destroying two aircraft. Fearful of another attack, the next day, the three unscathed battleships were moved further north to Naples. It took the Italians six months to repair the two damaged battleships. This attack significantly reduced the strength of the Italian naval fleet in the Mediterranean; it was a great victory, and the struggle for the Mediterranean had well and truly swung in the direction of British control.

Italian bombardments were winding down. Some 300 homes had been damaged or destroyed by the Italian raids. Many of the families that fled the Grand Harbour and surrounding towns returned to their homes. The reduction in air attacks and the impending winter months were the main factors behind this, as well as the assurance of underground shelters continuing to be dug in these locations. Government restrictions on shop closures were also removed, and it seemed that the lives of the Maltese were returning to some semblance of normality. It was estimated that more than 20,000 refugees would return to their homes by November.

In late November, the British launched another convoy operation to send supplies, ammunition and personnel. To avoid detection, the group of ships sailed close to the coast of North Africa. The merchant ships were flanked by seven destroyers and corvette battleships. The Italians spotted the convoy and closed in. They engaged in battle south of Sardinia for almost an hour. Allied dominance in the Mediterranean was evident; the Italians were hardly able to interrupt the convoy before retreating, and the convoy continued safely to Malta. The next day, however, as the convoy entered the Grand Harbour, the Italians launched a surprise air attack. Italian fighters unleashed a barrage of explosives over the merchant ships, but the attack was ineffective, causing only minimal damage. The ships docked safely and the cargo was unloaded, some 20,000 tons of it.

Meanwhile, Mussolini, having struggled to gain control of Malta, decided to invade Greece. Already occupying Albania, Mussolini then instructed his troops to enter bordering Greece without consulting Axis partner Germany. Hitler was not at all pleased about the ill-prepared move. He offered German troops to assist, but Mussolini declined, certain of a quick victory. However, it proved to be a strategic failure. After one week, not only had the Greeks repelled the

Italian invaders back into Albania, they also advanced deep into Albania and captured 5,000 Italian troops as prisoners. The winter had slowed advancement, and both sides were content to settle. The Italians spent the next few months in a defensive position against the Greeks. Greece was a neutral party to the war; however, the Axis invasion softened their stance to allow British intervention at Churchill's insistence. The Greeks accepted aircraft but asserted that British personnel be sent to protect Crete only. The Greeks were afraid that British troops on mainland Greece – continental Europe – would raise Hitler's ire. Churchill accepted the Greeks' instructions, seeing an opportunity to gain some ground near mainland Europe; Crete was in striking distance of the Romanian oil infrastructure that fuelled Germany's war efforts.

In early November, Hitler convened with the Foreign Minister of the USSR. He suggested a share arrangement with Germany after the war was won. The USSR was not interested in the pickings of a dissected British Empire, instead preferring that Germany honour the terms of the Nazi–Soviet Pact signed in August of 1939. The pact was an agreement of convenience between discordant parties, which permitted them to acquire supremacy of eastern Europe, while assuring that they would not attack each other for ten years. The Soviets made clear their own demands: the annexation of Finland, free movement in the Baltic north seas, and influence over the Balkan states of Bulgaria and Yugoslavia. Hitler left the meeting furious; the interaction hardened his resolve to pursue his plans to confront the Soviets. He was driven by his belief that for true German sovereignty to be achieved, eastern Europe must be subjugated – of course, this included the Soviet Union.

The Axis powers continued to grow in strength and number; on 20 November, Hungary officially joined the Tripartite Pact. Within the following days, Slovakia and Romania – countries that were ruled by fascist leaders – also joined the Pact.

President Roosevelt won an unprecedented third term in office. He was a popular choice among the people of America, still feeling the effects of the Great Depression and pleased with his handling of the war. He went on to win a fourth term in 1944, as the war was nearing its end. He was, and always will be, the only US President to serve more than two terms in office (an amendment was ratified in 1951 that limited presidents to two terms). Roosevelt's re-election meant that the British retained a strong supporter of the Allied cause. Churchill would continue to receive the assistance he needed to continue the fight against the ever-growing Axis powers.

A HAPPIER YEAR?

Journal entry: 25 December 1940

I did not guess that a wartime Christmas would be the most cherished Christmas I've ever had. The moments in life hitherto taken for granted are appreciated more than ever because they are endangered, threatened. Thankfully, the war clouds had dispersed in the lead-up; it's been four days since we've had to retreat under the menacing sound of the wailing sky, and today was no different. A sense of great relief has settled over the population; the pause in attacks has instilled an air of hope that hostilities are near their end, allowing us to enjoy the most revered day in our nation's calendar.

Yearly traditions that once felt tedious, I actually came to miss this year. The curfew meant restrictions on celebrations for the sake of safety. This year, no midnight mass followed by a procession and candlelight gathering in the square. Previously, I had participated more out of duty than desire; mother was pleased when father and I joined in with her. I think back fondly to those occasions now. I recall the shimmering glow of the collective firelight; we were encapsulated in a dome of yellow light, huddled closely to provide some warmth from the winter chill. The service would end with an a cappella rendition of 'Silent Night'. The choir would commence and the congregation would harmoniously lend their voices to the soothing carol to create such a charming ambience … it gives me goosebumps thinking about it now, and I regret taking such peaceful moments for granted.

This year, the mass was shortened and limited to daylight hours, with restrictions placed on singing. However, that didn't deter attendance: people standing around the perimeter, three bodies deep, the most I've ever seen. I felt encouraged by the sense of unity and determination, the people refusing to allow our oppressor to dampen their way of life. The priest announced an unfamiliar pre-mass warning – to immediately seek shelter if there was a siren – but thankfully the service was uninterrupted. One carol was allowed; what would otherwise resound at the top of our lungs was restricted to a low hush without organ accompaniment, in case the siren sounded. It happened to be my favourite carol ever since childhood! I didn't know why it resonated with me until I sung it today. I was struck with emotion when I sang the words 'peace on earth'. I realised that a harmonious humanity is something I've always innately wished for the world. And now that the situation on earth is anything but peaceful, I desired it all the more. I am grateful that, although we still lived under the shadow of war, I was able to celebrate this Christmas in relative peace at this time, when others throughout Europe and the world may not be as fortunate. It was the mildest performance of 'Hark the Herald Angels Sing' I've ever heard, but it certainly didn't lack strength of heart. As the singing progressed, it felt as though the atmosphere was filled with an inspiration that lifted our spirits – a moment I won't forget.

An afternoon Christmas feast was put on at Lascaris for the military families. We had spent so much time together the past six months, it was fitting that we celebrate together. Each family was to contribute by bringing a homemade dish. Mother and I were tasked with organising a dessert. Our favourite sweet Christmas treat came to mind – the traditional Christmas log – to me it wouldn't be Christmas without it! I had a refreshing time. Even though we were in the military headquarters, we didn't talk about the war; I even forgot about it for a time. There wasn't a grim face in the room and the children were ecstatic when Santa made an appearance. I think that brought the most joy for the adults, to see the children being children, without a care in the world. We left the celebrations early to beat the curfew, and to visit Uncle Tino and Auntie Angelina, and cousins Giuseppe and Theresa, like we do every Christmas. We hadn't seen them since before the start of the war. It was heartening to see they are well and keeping safe.

But the cheerful events of this day have reached a solemn ending, as I am reminded of a tradition that won't be fulfilled this year. Indeed, it has been marred for the remainder of my years. For the past four years, Louie, Helena, Maria, Joe and I have met in the fleeting hours of Christmas Day. A time to reminisce on the year past and think on the year ahead. While at the Christmas Party, I talked to people who'd had contact with them, I'm relieved to know they're all doing okay. It's the longest time we've ever been out of touch with each other. Louie and his mother bake bread for the people every day, Helena still teaches children despite the interruptions of the war, and Maria, well, she's created an ornate underground shelter for the people of her town. I chuckled when I heard that. I don't know if we'll recommence our gathering, but there will be an enduring emptiness in my heart for Christmas nights to come: the knowledge of never again sharing this moment with Joe. As a group, we did not give gifts to each other, but ever since childhood, Joe and I had. Last year's Christmas gift from Joe sits on my bedside table. A framed photograph of us taken at last year's summer fiesta. It was the first time I've been in a photo booth. It's special to me because it captures the four seasons of us: the serious, the silly, the jovial, and the unspoken affection.

The last six months of this year have been the most defining of my life. As the year fades and transforms into another, I've learned that I need not settle in the doldrums of perpetual sadness; sorrow and despair can be overcome by small inspirations of hope. For the nation, and myself, it's been an incredibly gruelling year, yet mixed with sporadic rays of light and the sparkle of promise for a new beginning and a brighter year ahead.

Here's to a happier year.

RS

Narrative: December 1940

In the six months since their first attack, the Regia Aeronautica had hardly dented the morale of the Maltese and was no closer to subduing the island. During this period, the RAF shot down 45 Italian aircraft and damaged almost 200 of their bombers and fighters, while incurring far fewer losses themselves. The year ended well for the Maltese people. Christmas was celebrated without interruption; in fact, there were no air raid sirens in the four days leading up to Christmas. The next siren would not sound until 29 December. The island continued to be replenished well; merchant ships were reaching Malta without hindrance. A few weeks earlier, submarines had arrived to bolster the arsenal of offensive vessels aiming to strike Axis shipping lanes between Sicily and North Africa. The successful delivery of supplies holistically reinforced the island: civilian supplies to maintain sustenance and improve health; military equipment, fuel, and a variety of British personnel including maintenance and RAF crews. In all, over 3,000 military men were now on the island. The reinforcement of military capabilities improved the island's position as an offensive base and ensured that it was better prepared against further attacks.

It was evident that when Malta was strengthened, so too were the British; they gained a stronger foothold in the Mediterranean and North Africa. The taming of the Regia Aeronautica allowed Allied military reinforcements and supplies to reach British posts in North Africa, giving British forces increased momentum against the Italians. At the start of December, the British halted the Italian advance into Egypt and by early January, Italian troops were completely driven out of Egypt; 34,000 Italian prisoners were captured in the process. The success of the British in North Africa was aided by attacks from Malta on Axis ships, causing losses of 50,000 tons of supplies. Throughout the opening weeks of January, further attacks on Libyan ports – Tripoli and Bardia – were conducted. The balance of the battle for sky and sea supremacy of the Mediterranean was well and truly with the Allied forces.

At this point, it seemed that the worst was over for the people of Malta. However, a greater threat loomed in the background, a more insidious belligerent that would cast an ominous shadow over the island. In fact, the taming of one beastly giant would summon another, greater beast. The ineffectiveness of the Italians in southern Europe initiated Hitler's involvement in the region. Germany's intervention in the Mediterranean arena was about to begin. The spirit and resolve of Malta and her people would be tested unlike anything it had ever experienced in its long history.

Meanwhile, Italy's military incompetence was becoming apparent. By the end of the year, Mussolini conceded his failure to annex Greece and accepted Hitler's offer of assistance; however, he rejected the offer to send German troops into Albania, afraid that Hitler would take control of the country. Hitler wished to secure southern Europe so he could focus on his planned attack on the USSR. Although approved, the surprise attack, codenamed Operation Barbarossa, would not take place until mid-1941.

THE LUFTWAFFE

Journal entry: 27 February 1941

An image has been seared onto the screen of my memory. Even now, in the momentary split second as I blink, the image is projected onto the back of my eyelids. All my preconceived notions of the world and humanity has been shifting during these war-filled months, but today… the foundation of all I believed has been struck with a severe hammer's blow – thrust in the air with no footing on which to land. And there I remain, in the wandering space of this chaotic reality.

This may sound like a strange thing to say, but how I wish the Regia Aeronautica was still bombing us; at least there was time to breathe. The Luftwaffe is a merciless beast devouring anything and everything in their path. Now I understand how Europe capitulated to the unrelenting, vehement conquest of the Nazi war machine, aggressively driven by the desire for dominance, not ceasing until supremacy is achieved. A profound terror has gripped the land, unlike that instilled by the Italians. The fear is evident in the people's preference to remain underground. Lascaris connects to the tunnels where they take refuge; their fear echoes through the narrow ways like a groaning ghost. During my daily visit through the shelters, an air raid siren triggered an instant hush, as though the air was sucked out of the room, the dread palpable. You would think being underground would bring a certain sense of security, but it didn't. It was but an anxious wait for the pummelling above to begin. Families huddled close together;

one young man sat in a foetal position, hands over ears, rocking back and forth. The hum of the Lord's Prayer was the underlying tone to the loudening rumble; it sounded like a swarm of 1,000 deadly bees approaching. The rat-ta-tat-tat of the gunners on the ground added to the cacophony of oncoming dread. The demonic shriek of the dive bombers sent a shiver to the bones, then the piercing sound at which we have all learned to fall down and tremble: the whistling deluge. The groans of terror intensified; we all anticipated the looming impact. The deep sound of the first assault instilled a nerve-racking tremor. It was as though Malta is a huge timpani, and the percussionist struck a blow with all his might; it then became incessant; wave after wave, they kept coming, a drum roll in quick succession. The ferocity of the strikes shook loose limestone dust from the ceiling, causing a light drizzle of sandy rain, making it harder to breathe in the already confined space. The ones that explode right above us cause a violent quake and provoke a chorus of whimpers, fearful the ceiling will tear apart and collapse upon us.

In the aftermath, there is a slight relief; the tension remains, though, knowing they'll return. Today, curious, I ventured to the surface for the first time after a fresh German bombardment. Tentative because of father's warnings, but he wasn't with me at the time. In hindsight, I wish I had heeded his advice. It was an eerie sight; the bitter winter gale carried away the thick plumes to reveal new destruction, the howl of the wind complimenting the haunting, gloomy scene. It was apocalyptic! Silence, apart from the continual crumbling of masonry; the lingering smoke haze tickled my throat. I felt disoriented; there was debris as far as I could see. Streets once lined by houses completely flattened, rubble everywhere, hardly a flat surface on which to step. A grey dust canopy hovered above; it was several minutes before I could see a sliver of blue sky. Others slowly emerged from the surrounding underground shelters and homes, like rabbits from their burrows. An elderly man caught my eye, coughing and covered in white dust, moving wearily from his damaged home. Then, in horror, he fixed his gaze on the house next to his. It had become a pile of displaced stones. He yelled, 'my neighbour, my neighbour's inside!' Everyone in the vicinity immediately rushed to climb the mound of rubble and form a line. The rescuers lost their sense of self-preservation, working frantically under precariously balanced masonry, while smaller rubble rained down around them. I was inspired to lend a hand. I hurried up the mound to start a new line, and others followed my lead. I felt as though I was moving stones twice my weight, in sync with my heartbeat. Then, the adrenaline rushing through me came to a shock-induced standstill … I felt something inside me depart, as though the last shred of my innocence was ripped from me. I stood there, still holding the stone I had just picked up, staring at the pale dust-covered lifeless hand I had uncovered. The person next to me tapped my upper arm for me to hurry. He then realised why I had paused in such a state of shock. He took the stone from me and passed it on. He guided me away by the shoulders and calmly repeated, 'it's okay, it's okay'. He left me to sit alone and returned to help. In my mind, I responded to his remarks, 'but it's not okay'. People are losing their lives due to someone's senseless quest for power. I knew of the casualties, I've experienced loss myself, but today it became tangible, the first time I saw clearly the fatal reality of war. The adolescent girl within, full of limitless dreams and youthful innocence, has skipped away into the shadows never to return, devoured by the evil realities of an ever-darkening, fallen world.

The haunting presence of the Luftwaffe has left a deep scar on our land and on the hearts of the people. Cutting ever deeper the longer we remain under its malevolent shadow. There is a distinct callousness to their presence that makes my hairs stand on end. The people feel it too, the distress written on their faces tells of the unspoken terror that we're dealing with an insidious wickedness like no other; the most heart-wrenching reality is that the Luftwaffe assault has only just begun.

RS

Narrative: January–March 1941

By the end of the first week of the new year, Hitler had amassed several Luftwaffe fleets stationed throughout various air bases in Sicily, preparing for Germany's campaign in the Mediterranean and North African region. From 9 January, the Luftwaffe presence was felt from their first incursion over Malta. Churchill's fear of their involvement in the Mediterranean had now become a reality. On that day, nine Junkers Ju 87 dive bombers, popularly known as the Stuka, attacked the southern Port of Marsaxlokk. The Stukas were specially designed to dive at a steep angle, releasing bombs at low altitude with greater accuracy and inflicting maximum damage. Reaching speeds of up to 340 kilometres per hour, the Stukas were fitted with Jericho Sirens beneath the aircraft; when the aircraft dived at full speed, into a vertical decent, a terrifying scream sounded ever louder as the aircraft approached land. The sound was effectively a psychological weapon that instilled panic in the population.

The Germans engaged in their first attack on an Allied convoy operation to Malta, which had begun three days earlier and was still en route. It comprised several merchant vessels surrounded by a special defence force that included the noted Axis target HMS *Illustrious*, the aircraft carrier that took part in the attack of Taranto. The first wave of Axis fighter bombers was the Regia Aeronautica; but fighters launched from *Illustrious* repelled the attack. Within two hours, the second wave approached – this time, the Luftwaffe, over 50 aircraft, comprising Stukas and Messerschmitt 109 fighters. The Messerschmitt was a versatile modern aircraft and one of the most superior fighter planes of the Second World War, reaching a maximum speed of 685 kilometres per hour – the backbone of the Luftwaffe. The fighter planes protecting the convoy were not able to hold back the Luftwaffe and a concentrated attack on *Illustrious* ensued. The aircraft carrier was pounded. In the space of a few minutes, over three tons of explosives hit *Illustrious*. The bombardment blew holes, ignited fires and damaged the landing strip; however, the engines remained relatively unscathed. The convoy continued its journey, while the aircraft, unable to land on the carrier, flew to Malta to refuel. Three hours later, sixty kilometres from Malta, a third wave of twenty Luftwaffe fighters and bombers approached. Air cover from Malta returned to deter the oncoming attack but was outnumbered four to one. They managed to shoot down several bombers but one made it through the air defence, dropping a half-ton bomb on the carrier and igniting a raging blaze on the ship. The Luftwaffe dispersed, assuming they had finished off *Illustrious*, but the vessel remained afloat and by evening was less than ten kilometres from Malta. A group of Italian bombers were spotted heading for the carrier, but they were fended off by anti-aircraft fire from the escorting destroyers, and *Illustrious* made it to port in the Grand Harbour. The concentrated attack on *Illustrious* meant that the merchant ships were relatively unscathed, with much of their cargo reaching Malta: ammunition supplies, boxed Hurricane fighters, potato seeds and various RAF personnel, including provisions to increase anti-aircraft defences. Thus, the arrival of the Luftwaffe in the region signalled a severe turn in the war for the Allies. Their presence jeopardised the resupply of Malta; future attempts to send convoys would once again be extremely hazardous.

On 16 January, the Luftwaffe began an air raid blitz over Malta at an unprecedented level, particularly on the harbour area where *Illustrious* remained; they were intent on destroying the carrier once and for all. Over seventy Stukas infested the skies above the Grand Harbour, each taking their turn during a one-hour period, diving as low as thirty or forty metres to drop their loads. Submarines stationed in the dockyard, a vital weapon against Axis ships, were taken out to sea and rested on the ocean bed to protect them from damage. The few Hurricanes on the island and anti-aircraft gunners did their best to lessen the destruction but this was an overwhelming task. After the raiders had dispersed and the dark billows lifted, amazingly, *Illustrious* remained again untouched. However, the three ancient cities of Vittoriosa, Senglea and Cospicua had been heavily bombed. The capital, Valletta,[4] founded and built in the 16th century by the Knights of St. John, had stood unharmed for centuries. However, it

---

[4] In 1980, Valletta was declared a UNESCO heritage site:
https://whc.unesco.org/en/list/131/

could not evade the destructive might of the Germans; streets were littered with debris and hundreds of homes were destroyed. Casualties were high because people had returned to their homes during the lull in the Italian attacks. The population of these cities once again fled to safer areas. On 18 January, the Luftwaffe returned and targeted the airfields of Luqa and Hal Far in a two-hour bombing raid. The airfields, stationed aircraft and surrounding amenities were destroyed, leaving only one functional runway.

In the early morning of 19 January, the Luftwaffe returned to the Grand Harbour determined to finish *Illustrious*. Almost 100 Stukas released their rage, this time comprising one-ton bombs rather than the standard half-ton bombs. Further damage was done to the dockyard and nearby buildings. *Illustrious* was not hit; however, a near miss did cause further damage to the vessel. On 23 January, *Illustrious* would be fit enough to set sail. Dockyard workers had worked non-stop for the past two weeks to make the carrier seaworthy once more. In the evening hours, *Illustrious* slipped out of the Grand Harbour with a small defensive entourage and made the journey to the safer port in Alexandria, arriving two days later for further repairs. The period of attack on the aircraft carrier was known as the Illustrious Blitz.

There would be more attacks on the Luqa and Hal Far airfields during late February and early March. In an attack in February, one of the original three Gloster Gladiators was destroyed, *Hope*, leaving *Faith* the sole survivor. As much as 100 Axis aircraft partook in a single raid, outnumbering the Maltese air defence ten to one. Planes were damaged on the ground; service buildings on the perimeters were destroyed. The village of Luqa bore the brunt of the attack, the majority of dwellings destroyed. However, this did not deter the residents. The near eighty per cent that lost their homes were taken in by their neighbours and continued on with life as best they could. On 9 March, there was a surprise attack on the third airfield, Ta' Qali. The constant attacks on the airfields limited Malta's air defence, and the aerial combat took a toll on the aircraft, now reduced to four. Planes were well worn and used far beyond their life span, patched up with spare bits and pieces, whatever they could find, not necessarily plane parts; parts such as propellers had to be made by dockyard workers due to lack of proper spares. It became apparent that, despite the valiance displayed by the RAF fighter pilots – making the best use of the equipment they had – in the short time since the Luftwaffe had entered the Mediterranean arena, they had swiftly dominated the skies over Malta and the Mediterranean.

Until the arrival of the Luftwaffe, supplies on Malta had been adequately replenished during the quieter months under the Regia Aeronautica. The Luftwaffe proved devastating for the Maltese people. In just over a week of their first strike, the island's gains were decimated. In February, there were 107 air raids and March endured 105; approximately 2,000 tons of explosives were dropped on Malta. The aim of the Luftwaffe was to break the people's morale – by bombing Malta into surrender. And bomb they did; the Luftwaffe would engage in a brutal aerial campaign in the opening months of the new year; air raid sirens sounded several times throughout the day and within the first three months, there was only one day without an air raid siren. Due to the lack of Malta-based aircraft, a large proportion of the air defence had to come from the ground, the anti-aircraft gunners scattered around the harbour. The intensity of attacks meant that the island's ammunition was desperately running low and required constant replenishment – if they were to continue to fight off enemy raiders. On 21 February, a convoy supply arrived safely from Alexandria, unnoticed by the Axis forces. It was a timely boost for the nation: over 1,000 troops, and many tons of supplies that included small tanks, various motor vehicles, armoury and the much-needed ammunition.

Hitler made a key appointment regarding his Axis expansion southward of mainland Europe: General Erwin Rommel to oversee the campaign in North Africa. Rommel recognised the strategic significance of Malta in the region: that the Allies were in close range to Axis supply and communication lines between Africa and Europe. Rommel stated that unless Malta was neutralised, Axis forces would ultimately lose control of the Mediterranean and North Africa. Rommel arrived in North Africa on 12 February; by the end of the month, the German position was gaining strength with troops and supplies reaching Tripoli. Their supply routes were hardly hindered due to Malta being pummelled, restricting Malta-based offensive strikes. The additional supplies equipped the Rommel-led Afrika Korps to prepare for an offensive push against British forces. At the time, the British had control of the eastern half of Libya and had made great gains against the Italians in Somaliland and Eritrea. However, the deteriorating situation on Malta left these gains under threat.

Meanwhile in mainland Europe, Hitler's influence and the Axis powers continued to grow. His continued pressure on the Bulgarian government to join the Axis alliance was finally successful. Hitler needed Bulgaria's compliance for a planned attack on Greece from within Bulgaria's borders. The British Government attempted to form an anti-Axis alliance in the Balkans. Yugoslavia and Turkey rejected their overtures; however, Greece was interested. The imminent invasion moved Greece to officially accept Britain's request to send troops; British and Australian troops landed in Greece from Egypt on 7 March.

6. The damaged ship bell of HMS Illustrious, which survived the blitz in January 1941.

HOLDING ON

Journal entry: 3 May 1941

The nightly wails have become a soundtrack throughout the land. Slumber rarely reaches the deep rest of serenity these days: rather, semiconscious, alert dozing. Hoards approach in waves throughout the nocturnal hours, like menacing bats, intent on disturbing the peace – and that they do. They linger in the sky to set off the sirens, interrupting any attempt at continuous rest. Sleep was once an escape from the realities of war, a brief respite from the chaotic waking hours. But that possibility has faded with the increased hostilities of the Luftwaffe's presence in recent months; their aggression has impressed grim visions of hellish destruction that remain alive and vivid even in dreams. It's no longer the sounds of war that disturb me; it's the nightmares that jolt me awake in a wheezing panic. Harrowing scenes of the annihilation of my family, my people, my country. The initial waking moment is terrifying; in that split second, it seems as though the end of the nightmare is my reality. Then comes the partly alleviating realisation that it was just an awful dream. These reoccurring visions have sparked an underlying fear of these nightmares coming to fruition. But there's one good thing to come from the disrupted nights – these dreams aren't given time to fester. Then again, the disruption has introduced another front of warfare, an attack on the psyche, mental torture to break the will of the people. It's taking a noticeable physical toll. When I look into the mirror, it seems

I've aged ten years in less than a year. The weariness of body and mind compound the already dire need for provisions, which diminish within days of arrival. The trickle from the carpet runs is indeed helpful but we need large ships of supplies, several times over. Yet I know that such convoy attempts would place merchant vessels as sitting ducks in a carnival shooting gallery, waiting to be picked off one by one.

The situation of my people is heading towards an outcome that appears far from promising. The malicious superpower holds this tiny opponent under its thumb, miles away from assistance and amidst a circumference of tempestuous enemies. The life-threatening storms pass over daily; each time, the landscape changes, another piece of my ancient capital disappears or is destroyed. Generational family homes, where decades of memories and ornaments have collected over time, are wiped away in a single air sweep. From a high point of Valletta, across the Grand Harbour, the place where the Three Cities once stood graceful for centuries was now unrecognisable. The years and intricate labour required to build such magnificent structures, which have witnessed hundreds of years of history, reduced to rubble in a few short moments. I wonder if there will be anything left of Malta's history by the end of this war. The gripping fear that the Luftwaffe instil in their wake has transformed into an increasing sense of indignation. The people are incensed by the senseless loss of life and widespread destruction, our unique and intrinsic cultural heritage incrementally wiped away wave by wave. The heart of the people is most struck by the damage to our centuries-old capital and the opulent St. John's Co-Cathedral; thankfully the damage so far is only minor.

The intent of the enemy to shatter the people has instead steeled our resolve. Despite their ongoing torment, the people do not utter the word 'surrender'. There is not a hint of giving in, even though it would alleviate our dreadful existence, leading to the cessation of bombing and plentiful supplies. Submission would mean willingly forfeiting our freedom and placing ourselves at the whim of the invaders. In one way, surrender may seem like the best outcome for the people, but there would be such stigma to come with it. It would be a lasting scar on the nation's soul, and a stain on the heart of every citizen. To give up the fight and bow down to the conqueror is not the Maltese way;

this nation has persevered in the past and it will persevere today! This nation is built on the people's resilience and thrives on a tenacious spirit that inspires every person and strengthens our collective heart. It is no wonder we have kept an imposing Goliath at bay so far. Enduring almost a year of fierce onslaught and we still maintain dominion of our land, while other nations – with larger populations and military capabilities – have crumbled in the face of the Axis forces in much less time. This is a resounding testament to the nation's toughness. We will press on despite the most challenging circumstances and I stand bravely with my people as we declare with our wills, 'we will continue to resist. We will continue to fight. Despite what is thrown at us, till the last gasp of this nation, we will keep holding on!'

RS

Narrative: April–May 1941

Malta remained the most exposed and vulnerable piece of land in the British Empire. The Luftwaffe took advantage of Malta's precarious isolation and was merciless in its attacks. Determined to crush morale and thrust the Maltese further into demoralisation, they targeted civilian towns on Good Friday and Easter Sunday (11–13 April). Malta, a deeply religious nation with longstanding traditions and a commitment to celebratory festivals during such holy days, was unable to practise its faith. However, the Luftwaffe campaign had the opposite effect to its intended purpose; it strengthened the resolve of the people to persevere through the menacing bombardments even though the situation on the ground was worsening. Valletta and the surrounding cities were shut down and strict curfews enacted. A rationing scheme was implemented to conserve dwindling stock. By mid-April, equipment and ammunition shortages had rendered several anti-aircraft guns useless; orders placed months ago were yet to be fulfilled. There was another refugee crisis, with over 12,000 left homeless; over 2,000 buildings, mostly homes, were reduced to rubble, with half of those in Valletta alone.

In April, Malta would endure its most intense bombing attack; for fifteen days straight from the 16th, over forty bombing raids were conducted. The night hours of the last two days of April were the most intense. In one instance, almost ninety Axis aircraft took part in a continuous attack that lasted over six hours. Throughout the two-week raid, parachute flares were used to illuminate the land at night; bombers dropped over 800 bombs, some weighing up to one ton. There was nothing that was not hit: airfields, towns, churches, homes, banks, shops, hospitals, museums, law courts, with the brunt of the daily attacks focused on the harbour area, Valletta and neighbouring cities.

Although under heavy attack, as much as possible, Malta remained a base for attacks on Axis vessels. The British War Cabinet was adamant that Malta must be equipped as a base for strikes against the Axis powers to lessen their influence in the region. Such offensive strikes had been minimal in recent times, allowing over 320,000 tons of Axis supplies to be sent to North Africa from Italy since the Luftwaffe's presence in the region: ninety-four per cent of supplies reaching their intended destination. To counter these Axis gains, a flotilla, a small sea fleet of four destroyers, was sent to Malta to form a strike force. In April, the flotilla attacked a German convoy departing Naples to Tripoli. All five ships were destroyed or damaged and 12,000 tons of Axis supplies lost.

Sending supplies to Malta had been reduced to carpet runs: supply deliveries via submarine. This was the safest method and went mostly unnoticed by Axis forces. These small yet vital deliveries proved pivotal in maintaining Malta's longevity and the wellbeing of civilians in the absence of substantial convoy deliveries via ships. Various supplies, deemed most crucial at the time, were packed into every nook and cranny, with shipments sent every few weeks. These clandestine supply runs would continue for several months, most often during those periods of heavy bombardment. When possible, attempts were made to send a greater quantity of supplies. By month's end, a troop ship from Alexandria made it to Malta safely; as well as carrying fuel and various stores, it was particularly successful due to a diversionary attack on Tripoli. At the start of May, Malta received its largest supply convoy to date. It was part of a major operation that involved the entire Allied Mediterranean fleet to transport supplies from Gibraltar to Egypt and Egypt to Gibraltar – making a drop on Malta. Bad weather and mist provided a natural cover for the vessels on their journey; however, the convoy endured minor attacks and sea mines proved a hindrance, with one supply ship sinking after hitting two mines, losing its main cargo of tanks and Hurricanes. In all, 30,000 tons were delivered, mostly military supplies, oil and stores. By the end of the month, Malta would receive over fifty aircraft from Gibraltar, adding to the forty-five aircraft received in prior weeks. This replenishment of supplies and aircraft rejuvenated the island's position. Malta's recent fortune coincided with a large contingent of the German air fleet being moved from Sicily to the Balkans in preparation for Hitler's planned invasion of the USSR.

The Luftwaffe had asserted their dominance in the region; Malta had been subdued while Axis forces had increased their territory in North Africa. The Afrika Korps had pushed back the British troops into Egypt, within ten kilometres of the Egyptian border.

Meanwhile, Yugoslavia joined the Tripartite Pact on 25 March; two days later, the government was overthrown. The new government made haste to show its preferred allegiance with the USSR and Britain. This enraged Hitler and he ordered an invasion, comprising German, Italian and Hungarian troops; by mid-April, Yugoslavia would be conquered. Greece would follow; Allied forces were unable to counter the push of Axis forces, evacuating almost 20,000 troops and suffering heavy naval loses. Greece was lost to Axis control and an airborne invasion of Crete was successful, the island falling into Axis hands by the start of June. This would mean an Axis base in the eastern Mediterranean, close to the Middle East and Egypt, threatening the safer option of eastern convoy supplies from Alexandria to Malta. The complete Axis control of the Balkans was now complete. With Egypt on the verge of being swallowed up by Axis forces, and with the entire mainland continent of Europe (excluding the neutral countries) now under the rule of Hitler, Malta had never been more isolated or surrounded – it lay a bullseye waiting to be targeted.

A NEW SEASON

Journal entry: 28 September 1941

Another day to cherish, such sweet seasonal relief. I'm seeing the world with renewed eyes and a grateful heart, treasuring every moment of relative calm. The alleviation amongst the people is tangible; the weight of an overbearing darkness has been lifted from our lives and a more cheerful countenance has settled. The period of terrorising skies endured, with its pelting gusts and surging cold-heartedness; we held on with hopeful endurance till the storm clouds parted and made way for a new season of life, the terrifying gusts now reduced to a brief puff of wind. As with the natural seasons of the weather, so too, the seasons of life change. Still it rains, but the torrent has eased to a manageable shower. The frantic pounding drums have slowed to a periodic beat that hardly provokes our collective dread. We welcome the presence of the Regia Aeronautica if it means the Luftwaffe stays away. Although the siren sounds the same regardless of which enemy air force approaches, our reaction to the sirens is quite different. Under the Luftwaffe, the sound instilled a gripping sense of panic and dread, as everyone scrambled for cover. Under the Regia Aeronautica, the people hardly flinch, continuing to go about their business. In fact, many even stop to watch the aerial action – almost as though being entertained by an air show!

The strangling threat that restricted substantial supply convoys is also loosening, lifting the island from the drought. Today's arrival of goods is the largest yet! The masses flocked to the harbour to cheer it home. The jubilant sounds were a welcome change from sirens, ammunition rounds and the buzz of aircraft. We may not have won the war, but this was certainly a victory for the nation. I feel there is a connection between today's provision and the National Day of Prayer declared a few weeks ago. The Luftwaffe was summoned elsewhere at just the right time, when the nation was on its knees. Their absence allowed the recent flow of replenishments to reach the island mostly untouched – at a dire time, the nation gasping for air.

However, I'm sure the island's resurgence will place Malta on Hitler's radar again. No doubt our persistence will be perceived as a provocation by the Nazis; a hindrance to their drive to wholly dominate via coercion and brute force. They have shown their desire not to let anything prevent them fulfilling the goals of their covetous hunger. They even desire conflict with larger opponents – the Soviet army is more than double that of the Germans! They surely won't tolerate hindrance from a small island, with hardly any armed forces. To them, Malta must seem an annoying piece of white lint that sticks out against their mission to cloak the world under their dark banner. They're determined to eliminate any speck of defiance against their charge to spread their crimson cape from the top of mainland Europe down to Africa; Malta remains the only obstruction that shines its light through their all-consuming darkness. To my mind, their red banner is symbolic of the blood on their hands.

I don't know what tomorrow will bring, but I know life will progress through its seasons. Each season of life is another colourful mosaic piece contributing to the overall make-up of a person; this can be said of the nation too. We have been through a time of uprooting, a time of tearing down, a time of weeping. This current season is a time to recoup, a time to embrace this season of life, a time to gather stones for the next battle. As we hover through this unknown phase of war, we prepare for what may come. We endured through the last blustering winter by the skin of our teeth, still vigilant of a more demanding winter season to come …

RS

Narrative: June–October 1941

The besieged island of Malta had survived its first year of war. By June, the Mediterranean skies were free of large units of Luftwaffe aircraft; it was believed they had completed the job of neutralising the island. Their dominance was evident: pulverising the landscape, diminishing the people's quality of life, convoy supplies kept at bay, and aircraft stocks decimated – many destroyed on the ground at airfields. Malta simply was not militarily equipped to keep up with their destructive supremacy. During the Luftwaffe's short presence in the region, Axis territory surrounding Malta had expanded; the Mediterranean southern coastline now stretched from Spain to Turkey, and the North African coastline from Morocco to within Egypt.

Now, the reigns to keep Malta subdued and maintain supremacy in the region were handed back to the Italians. The British considered the absence of the Luftwaffe a time of relative reprieve and a prime opportunity to bolster the island's offensive and defensive capabilities. Churchill reiterated his esteem for Malta and the strategic importance of the island, regarding Malta as one of the master keys of the British Empire.[5] He would make haste to ensure the longevity of the island's military capabilities and its people, should another onslaught occur in the future.

The Italians conducted air raids, but these attacks paled in comparison to the intensity of the Luftwaffe's attacks. Air raids fall to their scarcest since the start of the war, sometimes to once a day. The potency of the Regia Aeronautica was shrugged off and plans to rejuvenate the island were under way: vital repairs to key infrastructure, replenishment of civilian and military supplies, repairs to equipment and aircraft, and the clearing of sea mines around the harbour.

A new air command officer was stationed on Malta. An inspection of the airfields revealed the dire situation. The number of aircraft available was less than expected. Repairs were difficult due to scarcity of parts; even basic tools such as wrenches and hammers were difficult to come by. The airfields and aircraft shelters were small and

---

[5] https://timesofmalta.com/article/When-the-plight-of-Malta-obsessed-him.491352

insufficient; most aircraft remained on the runways, making them easy targets. In time, the air command officer would improve these deficiencies to better protect the air fleet, building pens and walls to protect the aircraft and a sheltered facility underground for repair workers.

Over 100 Hurricanes were sent to the island throughout June, which commenced a consistent wave of offensive strikes on bases in Italy and North Africa, including Axis convoys. Targets such as military bases and warehouses, harbours, ports, dockyards, storage facilities, electrical stations, railway lines, airfields, vehicles, aircraft, sea vessels, merchant ship and oil tankers were damaged or destroyed, including several thousand tons of merchant supplies. Attacks were conducted on the Italian and Sicilian cities of Naples, Palermo and Syracuse; in North Africa, Tripoli, Khoms, Sirte, Surman and Zuwara. The attacks forced the Axis forces in the Mediterranean on the back foot and gave the British planned convoy operation to Malta a clearer passage by taking out some of their bases and strike weapons.

In July, a substantial supply convoy to Malta called Operation Substance departed Gibraltar. As expected, the Regia Aeronautica attacked, causing minor damage and the loss of one ship, but the operation was ultimately successful. Almost 60,000 tons of supplies reached port: much-needed ammunition, kerosene, medical and food supplies, including additional anti-aircraft guns. The Italians attempted to disrupt the unloading of cargo in the Grand Harbour by sending a small group of naval vessels during the dark dawn hours of the 26th. When they reached the vicinity of the harbour gunners, they were met with a volley of anti-aircraft and large artillery gun fire from the harbour defence force, operated mostly by the Maltese. It took just over five minutes to decimate the oncoming attack, rendering their surprise attack utterly ineffective. This was the Italians' most embarrassing moment in their fight against Malta, indeed of the war – Malta, a mere minnow by comparison in every way possible, particularly in terms of military might, had been able to overwhelm a so-called world power.

In mid-to-late August, offensive attacks continued on Axis bases and shipping. A week-long operation inflicted major damage and destroyed 45,000 tons of Axis shipping. The island continued to be reinforced; another forty-five Hurricanes were sent and, with the ample aircraft, the RAF asserted their dominance in the skies once again. Bombers completely destroyed a 6,000-ton military supply ship. And now, when Italian fighters approached the island, they were met by an equal number of aircraft; the Italian fighters suffered the brunt of air contests. In one instance, the Regia Aeronautica lost eleven aircraft while only downing two. Malta-based attacks continue throughout September; submarines sink two of three merchant and troop ships from mainland Italy to Tripoli, adding to the woes of the Axis North African campaign, the balance of which was once again swinging back to favour British forces.

By the end of the month, the largest supply convoy operation to Malta would take place: Operation Halberd, comprising nine merchant ships carrying over 80,000 tons of supplies with an escort of 27 battleships, cruisers and destroyers. Italian raiders would make several attempts to disrupt the convoy, again to minimal effect; ultimately, all but one merchant ship made it to Malta to great fanfare. The island's strength had greatly improved over the last four months due to an influx of civilian and military supplies, while restricting the enemy's movement in the region and attacking Axis positions – destroying almost fifty Axis vessels, a loss of over 150,000 tons of Axis supplies. Due to the intense, effective Allied attacks, it was deemed too dangerous for Axis convoys to travel through the Mediterranean; supply attempts were put on hold for a time from mid-October.

Elsewhere in Europe, on 22 June, German troops entered the USSR, the launch of Operation Barbarossa. Thus, Hitler broke the non-aggression pact he had signed with Stalin in 1939. The invasion incorporated over 3,000 tanks and more than three million German troops split into three battalions making their way towards Leningrad, Moscow and Stalingrad. In one day, German troops were eighty kilometres inside the USSR border. By the start of July, they had captured Riga and Minsk.

Japan was also making its presence felt on the world war stage. In July, its forces established bases in southern Indochina, in addition to having pressured Vichy France the previous year into ceding bases in northern Indochina. The development concerned Roosevelt as this threatened the US-held territory of the Philippines and the Allied territories of Burma, Malaya and East Indies. America took a pre-emptive step in freezing Japan's assets and enforcing an oil embargo. The move threatened Japan's dominance in the region as they relied heavily on oil imports. Due to fear of becoming a subjugated state, the Japanese pressed on with plans to attack, seizing the oil by force.

In early August, the USA sent lend-lease assistance to the USSR, including arms and equipment to aid their fight against the Germans. In the same month, Churchill and Roosevelt met in Newfoundland, Canada. They agreed that the downfall of Nazi Germany was of utmost importance and created the Atlantic Charter. This outlined the following four freedoms: freedom of speech, freedom of worship, freedom from want and freedom from fear. This would become the basis for the creation of the United Nations in future years. Roosevelt remained adamant that the USA could not partake in military action against Germany; however, he would continue to support Britain.

By October, German troops occupied the whole eastern territory of the USSR from the sea of Azov in the south to the Gulf of Finland in the north, with Leningrad and Moscow in close range. The Germans were declaring their dominance to the world.

THEY RETURN

Journal entry: 31 December 1941

Entering the countdown of another wartime year, the beat of the enemy is again the soundtrack of this years' occasion. I recall finishing last year in relative ease with the hope that the worst may have been over. This year's end began with an upsurge of aggression, signalling the commencement of another arduous period. As I dreaded, the resurgence of our nation has provoked the wrath of the vile brute once again. The fearful anticipation is palpable; the demons of the sky have returned, this time with an absolute resolve to, once and for all, crush this bothersome little crumb that has continued to interrupt the antagonist's plans for world domination. Solemnity has gripped our hearts; we know the ruthless annihilation of which they're capable and their hunger to unleash a torrent of terror until subjugation is achieved. What is most daunting is that we have only just experienced the very beginning of their second coming. We sit in helpless waiting for the full force of the belligerent beast to pounce, attempting to devour us whole.

A caged underground existence is fast becoming the new norm. All-night barrages again, a sly tactic of the enemy to deprive the masses of sleep. The nightmares that lived in my dreams are now just as real in my waking hours; there's no escape from this beastly war. It's five till midnight and most are awake; heavy heads doze off but are jolted by another earth-moving explosion from nearby shelling –

sounds as though Ta' Qali air base took another hit. I'm amazed how mother remains unmoved in her slumber during the sporadic quakes beneath the Basilica (aptly named Sanctuary Basilica) as the townsfolk of Mosta take refuge beneath the grand structure. Exhaustion has never been more apparent, the dim candlelight revealing the shadow-lines of weariness on the faces as I glance around. None more telling than the fatigue of father's countenance. I worry for him; he bears a burden that has hunched him over, as though he carries a gigantic weight. He practically lives at Lascaris these days; I'm glad I can keep an eye on him when I'm there.

A countdown just began from a small group of revellers. The situation doesn't call for any type of celebration, but it seems to change the mood as others join the countdown chorus, 'three … two … one … Happy New Year!' A sole party horn sounded amidst the somewhat lacklustre cheer. I didn't join in, but it brought a smile to my face; I admire the people's will to continue living in these moments despite the dreadful reality we face.

Reflecting on the year past, it's been a rollercoaster of extremes. The promising beginning quickly faded into the depths of hopelessness, the wills of the people never more tested. Unexpectedly, though, the sky parted to reveal the dawn of an uplifting season, imparting a renewed breath … much like a weary rock thrush that had been strengthened by cumulative rejuvenation over time; first the faded blue plumage regained its vibrancy, then a flutter of the wings and a shaking off the dust, as it gained more potency, rising and launching from the ashes, reaching the peaks of heaven to overcome the assault of the enemy, and to attack them. However, the incremental rise to the mountaintop turned in a single moment, a rapid decent, crashing down in the instant of the Luftwaffe's return. I'm afraid to contemplate what this New Year will bring; an ominous sense has taken residence within that the downward decent will not stop at the bottom we have already seen, but will continue to spiral into the depths of the darkest abyss yet.

The nation's resolve has undoubtedly been hardened, having endured the first wave of relentless assault. This has proved a pertinent preparation for an impending second wave, accompanied by an eerie discomfort. I fear that this time an ever darker and fiercer storm gathers in the distance. I do hope, with every fibre of my being, that I am wrong.

RS

Narrative: November–December 1941

By late October, the island's health and military capabilities were at their strongest since their entry into the war. Malta had amassed almost 200 aircraft, including Hurricanes and various bombers; a further group of Royal Navy vessels were sent to form a second potent strike force flotilla. Anti-aircraft guns throughout the country had amassed to 1,400, with thousands of Royal military personnel and almost 4,000 civilians taking part in military operations. Crucially, there were adequate food stocks to last several months.

The success of Malta-based air and sea attacks proved effective; there were no Axis convoys seen in the Mediterranean for several weeks. The British had re-established their stronghold in the Mediterranean as well as in North Africa, while the Axis campaign was rapidly deteriorating. In need of urgent supplies, in the last week of November, a desperate attempt was made to send several Axis merchant ships to North Africa. They were spotted by the strike force and all were destroyed, including a fuel ship. A couple of days later, Malta launched a bombing raid on several bases in North Africa, further disrupting Rommel's Afrika Korps. In the second half of 1941, over sixty per cent of Axis ships were sunk. This was a devastating blow for Axis forces, severely weakened and on the verge of retreating altogether, while British forces had regained the territory of eastern Libya.

The strategic importance of Malta became even more evident; whoever had control of Malta held dominance of the Mediterranean region and North Africa. Hitler was irate over the apparent inability to overcome the Allied resistance in the Mediterranean and became personally involved. He ordered some Luftwaffe air fleets from the eastern front to return to Sicily and half of the Atlantic submarine fleet to be sent to the Mediterranean. He removed the Italian command and placed German Air Field Marshal Albert Kesselring in control of all operational Mediterranean forces, including the Regia Aeronautica. Hitler's intent was clear; he could have ordered the Luftwaffe air units to North Africa to regain territory lost, but he knew that the true source of the Axis woes was the small island nation of Malta, perched in the middle of the Mediterranean, proving to be a persistent interruption to Axis dominance in the region.

What looked to be a prosperous end to the year changed in early December with the return of the Luftwaffe. If Malta could not be taken by force, it would be beaten into submission. The plan was to starve the island of outside assistance, after which a planned invasion would follow. On the last day of November, Malta endured its 1,000th air raid alert. The following day, Kesselring arrived in Sicily to begin a clear mandate to neutralise Malta. The Luftwaffe made their presence felt immediately: air raid sirens sounding for hours on end, bombing raids intensifying and aircraft outside airfield pens being targeted. The RAF piloted the Hurricanes well but were no match for the superior German aircraft. The more advanced Spitfire was needed: an aircraft in the Allied arsenal that could match the Axis aircraft fleet. The Spitfire could reach a top speed of 575 kilometres per hour and was the aircraft of choice for the RAF. The request had been made but Malta had to wait until such aircraft would be available.

Offensive strikes from Malta continued for the first three weeks of December and were able to keep Axis convoy supplies at bay and target Axis bases. However, the continual Axis bombardment caused much damage and destruction to their military strike; by the end of the year, Malta and the British had once again lost their dominance in the region. The Italians launched an attack on Royal Navy ships in Alexandria, causing significant damage. The Malta-based naval strike forces were targeted and made near redundant; these hits limited the British naval presence in the region. In one twenty-four-hour period, three-quarters of the day was spent under air raid alert. More sea mines were deployed around the Grand Harbour entrance to lock in the Royal Naval fleet. Up to 100 aircraft would partake in daily raids on airfields, the Grand Harbour and key locations. The intensity of the Luftwaffe's return was telling; at the end of November, Malta endured seventy-five air raids and thirty-five hours under air alert. By the end of December, these had increased to 170 air raids and 200 hours under air alert.

The Luftwaffe's air supremacy paved the way for supplies to reach Axis ports with minimal interruption, reviving their position in North

Africa. The Afrika Korps was beginning to push back British forces from eastern Libya. Dominance in the region had well and truly swung back to Axis powers. The Allied position in the Mediterranean, North Africa and the Middle East was jeopardised more than ever with Axis powers determined to gain control of Malta once and for all. The return of the Luftwaffe began a bombing campaign that would thrust the Maltese people into their most devastating period; they would experience a pummelling the world had never seen before.

Elsewhere, on 7 December, Japan launched a pre-emptive strike against the USA, destroying their Pacific fleet based in Honolulu, Hawaii. Japan mirrored the British attack on Taranto a year earlier; further, it became their blueprint for the attack on Pearl Harbour. An immense attack involving six aircraft carriers launching over 350 aircraft, it destroyed almost 190 aircraft; 19 war ships were destroyed or damaged, over 2,400 people were killed and nearly 1,200 wounded. The next day, President Roosevelt addressed Congress, he called the attack on Pearl Harbour 'a date which will live in infamy' and declared war on Japan. Thus, the USA officially joined the Second World War. With their involvement, the war had become global and the largest the world had ever experienced. Britain joined the USA in declaring war on Japan; on the 11th, Germany and Italy declared war on the USA. Prior to the attack on Pearl Harbour, Roosevelt had maintained a passive stance due to strong public opinion, despite feeling otherwise himself. Following the attack, public sentiment changed dramatically, with over ninety-five per cent of the nation in support of the war against Japan. Hitler was delighted by Japan's actions and, due to their proactive involvement, was adamant that the Axis powers would win the war.

Later in the month, Roosevelt and Churchill met in Washington DC to discuss war efforts. Although the US War Cabinet leaned towards a focus on the Pacific arena, Roosevelt maintained the agreement he had made when he first met Churchill in Newfoundland – that Nazi Germany must fall. Not since the fall of France did Britain have such a powerful ally to fight with against growing Axis powers. At the time the USA entered the war, their military capabilities and stockpiles were not as powerful as the Axis powerhouses. However, they certainly had the most potential. The USA was the greatest power in the world when it came to wealth, manufacturing and local resources; and, in time, their full potential would be revealed.

On 1 January, 26 nations currently at war with the Axis powers met in Washington DC to become signatories of the Atlantic Charter created by Roosevelt and Churchill, all pledging an Allied allegiance against the Axis forces.

THE DOWNPOUR

Journal entry: 2 March 1942

Giants have besieged the land; no parcel nor lot have they not trod with their explosive thuds. The shrilling descent, no matter how many times we've heard the sound before, instils an anxious terror; the perpetual high-pitched shriek has left a permanent ring in our ears. Their thunderous steps cause the ground to shiver; their imprint carves a craterous scar on the land; their passage leaves crumbling wreckage in its wake. We are living the same awful day on repeat; tyrannical goliaths make their daily stroll through our island as though addicted to it; they devour what lies ahead of them; and again, return when hungry for more destruction. They come as determined hunters, not necessarily targeting the inhabitants, but making a bullseye of this patch of lonely land. Like rabbits fearing the hunter, the people squeeze into underground holes and tunnels, filling the corridor spaces, which, holding double the suggested capacity, makes underground living conditions all the more uncomfortable than before. What once were temporary shelters have now become permanent underground towns; the tunnels have been dug out parallel to the streets, the names of the streets above carved on the walls below. Scores of families have claimed dimly lit passageways or nooks as their own, setting up house and home with whatever items they could retrieve from their homes. It's a morbid existence but given the circumstances, it's simply safer to live underground than risk living above.

A new batch of supplies arrived from a carpet run; a few of the girls and I made our rounds to the adjoining tunnels and rooms. There's never enough for everyone, so we seek out the most despairing. I no longer wince at the offensive stench as I enter the tunnels; my olfactory sense numbed by the unique waft that has become more pungent over time. The foul air has a lingering aftertaste, impressed on the palate for years to come; the musty air is coupled with the perspiration of a thousand people and a hint of excrement, greeting me like a warm wet towel wrapping around me. It's not the people's fault, having been forced to live in dank conditions some thirty metres beneath the surface without proper ventilation. The perpetual pong, the candle smoke and falling dust from the ceiling have made a toxic concoction; the symphony of coughing reveals the chronic lung conditions of many. No running water to maintain cleanliness and hygiene, and the lack of proper sustenance weakens immune systems; perfect conditions for disease to flourish, and flourish it does. Pale skin marked with irritable pink blotches. Redness glows around the eyes of the feverish. Dripping perspiration glistens on gaunt faces in the candlelight. Now that I think about it, the scene resembles an underground lair for the untouchable. The only benefit to living underground, apart from keeping us safe from bombardment, is that we remain warm during the winter months. But the humidity raises other issues; everything is damp, causing mildew to fester. This compounds illness and respiratory problems. During bombing breaks, some of the underground population surface for a swift dose of Mediterranean air. The air above ground is filled with dust but it's still better than the stale air underground; mattresses and clothes are also brought up, in the hopes of preventing the reek of mildew or freckles of mould.

I'm never more content than when I'm relieving the needs of others. A bandage roll or a tin of sardines are received as though I was handing over 10,000 pounds. This morning, not even an hour had passed when I all but ran out of supplies; one egg remained that today could fetch up to one month's wages! I followed the moaning cry of a child and was led to a young mother with her two children nestled in the corner of the faintly lit room. A newborn slept on her folded legs while she attempted to calm her starving toddler. I crouched down in front of her, reached into my bag and handed her the egg. Her appreciation shone in her eyes. The toddler's crying subsided at the sight of the egg. I left them but remained in the darkened distance. The toddler watched intently as the mother cracked an opening in the egg and handed it to him. He grabbed the egg with both hands and fed on the contents as though drinking from a bottle.

Such occasional instances of serenity amidst the ugliness tug at the heart. Like during the brief calm between bombardments, the harmonious murmur of prayers rises to the fore. It's always there, it's just drowned out by the hellish noise above. It drifts in the air, a comforting lullaby. The sound complements the ambience of the candlelight glow, quietening the soul even if for a moment. I closed my eyes and felt transported by the collective prayers, forgetting where I was; it made my hairs stand on end. Words softly spoken resounded off the walls with a powerful yet gentle strength that lifted the spirit. A near-heavenly experience despite the ominous evil that surrounds us. Even more amazing was that the uttered prayers weren't for each person's self, rather for the ones who were fighting the enemy, protecting our land. For a time, I was lost in that ethereal moment but then quickly reminded of reality when another siren sounded, drowning out the heartening whispers.

I'm in awe of my people and their persistent hope in a seemingly hopeless situation. Not only do they face an outward battle against an aggressor to stay alive; there's the added inner battle to keep living, when the physical body is denied the necessary provisions. Such lack leads to misery, which attacks the mind and the will; and if that breaks, so does the heart of the nation. Every day we're thrust into a more meagre existence, our endurance tested unlike anything experienced before. Another day, another piece of sky falls on this nation. A dogged, hostile horde impedes all attempts at the replenishment we so desperately need. Trickles of supplies are indeed a blessing but pale in comparison to that which would alleviate the aching misery of the multitudes. The plight of the people inches ever closer to the gates of a hellish abyss. A nation on its knees and a waning morale perched on a knife's edge – the last straw could fall on us at any moment.

This winter season, called by the people the Black Winter, has been the most unrelenting. The blustering destructive winds blow their fiercest; the brutal cold, its bitterest bite; the pelting metal rain, its most damaging. Though we are daily knocked down, we're yet to receive the knockout blow. The continual fight remains, if it is even a fight. We're throwing pebbles at a seemingly impenetrable ironclad mammoth. Our resistance has been reduced to that of a dragonfly trying to hold back an eagle fixed on its prey. Our firm presence has been diminished to that of a beetle standing in the way of a wild boar. Will it ever end? It could … if we surrender! Pain and suffering are etched on the faces around me, but I also see the obstinate resolve that speaks louder; not a single word is heard of giving up. So I stand with the defiant heart of the nation and, together, we will embrace the downpour!

RS

Narrative: January–March 1942

In the first week of the New Year, the Luftwaffe launched a continuous thirty-six-hour raid over Malta, after which a retaliation strike was conducted on Castelvetrano airfield in Sicily; intelligence had showed numerous aircraft located there. The strike was a success, destroying over forty Axis aircraft. The attack was met with an immediate response, mainly targeting the airfields. The aim was to destroy planes on the ground and render airstrips unusable. Without functioning runways, bombers could not launch offensive strikes and fighters could not deter attacks in the air. The runway damage was minimal due to the solid rock beneath, leaving craters only thirty to fifty centimetres deep; these were promptly filled. The airfields of Luqa and Hal Far were worst hit; Axis bombers released one-ton bombs for maximum damage. The intense bombardment of the airfields required more repair men; 3,000 military and civilian men across the three airfields worked around the clock to ensure swift repairs; the only equipment available were hand tools, no machinery apart from lorries.

The increase in air attacks depleted the anti-aircraft ammunition stocks at an unexpected rate. Urgent requests were heeded; a small fast single-ship run was made, unnoticed from Alexandria, carrying ammunition. Overall, supplies were being exhausted rapidly; an urgent convoy supply was needed. Later in the month, a small supply convoy arrived from Alexandria. The convoy reached RAF air cover before being set upon, but the RAF was able to ward off the enemy raiders. It was a timely arrival: the first substantial convoy since Operation Halberd in September, consisting of over 20,000 tons of military and civilian supplies; it would ensure that the island remained afloat for several more weeks. Convoy supplies were crucial to Malta's longevity both militarily and for the civilians as there were very few local resources. Their only chance of survival relied heavily upon the outside world. Malta produced only approximately thirty per cent of its required food supply, reduced further by the impact of war; a constant supply was required if the island's people were to survive. By the end of the month, a total of 260 air raids were conducted.

Malta's situation was about to become far worse, with more Axis bombing fleets relocated to Sicily from Europe and North Africa. Throughout February, over 2,800 sorties were flown over Malta. In one instance, a Grand Harbour raid including the airfields lasted one hour; 150 high explosive bombs were dropped – one bomb dropped every twenty-four seconds. A new weapon in the Axis arsenal emerged: time bombs, set to explode after a time lapse. This placed the bomb disposal teams and civilians in perilous danger. Anti-aircraft gunners were advised to conserve ammunition, given strict instructions regarding when to fire. A desperate attempt to send supplies to Malta was scuttled. None of three supply vessels from Alexandra made it to the island. Two were sunk while one turned away due to the incessant attacks, the escorting destroyers no match for the fierce aerial bombardment. The Germans discovered the Manoel Island submarine base and launched daily attacks, causing much damage to submarines and the base. The attacks became so intense that the submarines were withdrawn from the island, removing one of the most effective weapons against Axis convoys.

At the beginning of March, Malta spent consecutive days constantly under a shower of bombs. In the period from the dawn of 3 March to the dawn of 7 March, the island endured sixty-four hours of bombing, the longest continuous period being thirty-three hours. The number of aircraft on the island dwindled; only a few Hurricanes remained serviceable. The Hurricanes were simply outclassed by the German aircraft. However, by the end of the first week of March, Malta's request for Spitfires would be realised. The Spitfire was a more advanced aircraft than the Hurricane, equalling the Messerschmitt; for the first time, Malta possessed aircraft that matched the Luftwaffe forces. It was a promising development, but Malta needed much more military might than fifteen Spitfires against the Luftwaffe's hundreds. However, the Spitfires' impact was immediately evident; on the 9th, a counterattack was able to mostly prevent a raid comprising ninety-four Luftwaffe aircraft, causing it to suffer several losses.

The RAF and anti-aircraft gunners on the ground contended well in the skies above Malta. The anti-aircraft gunners had gained a reputation for their accuracy. Axis pilots were flying higher to avoid them while some had withdrawn from approaching the island; even dive bombers had been deterred from swooping down so low in the daylight hours – but the Luftwaffe would not retreat. In response to Malta's recent Spitfire success, the Germans returned in greater numbers, with heavier bombardments. On 15 March, the capital was heavily bombed. Among the usual arsenal of bombs, for the first time, the Luftwaffe was armed with a six-by-one-metre, nearly two-ton bomb, dubbed the 'Satan' bomb. In all, fifteen tons of explosives fell on Valletta that day; after Vatican City, it is the second smallest European capital at only 0.61 square kilometres.

The Luftwaffe were unyielding in their attempts to wipe out Malta's airfields. The Stukas would release their bombs, then the Messerschmitts would follow, flying as low as twenty metres above the surface, machine-gunning anything and everything in their path. More pens were needed to protect the aircraft. Sandbags and barrels were used, filled with the rubble from damaged buildings and what were once people's homes. Between enemy raids, the people would scramble to their assigned positions to recommence construction of the pens and fill in the newly formed craters, making the runways serviceable once again. On 20 and 21 March, Ta' Qali airbase became the most bombed Allied airfield in the world. The Germans were convinced that Ta' Qali was the base for Malta's aircraft. In the space of a thirteen-hour period, an unprecedented barrage was unleashed. Two separate raids were conducted; during the first, 100 tons of bombs were dropped. The second raid consisted of over 200 bombers releasing over 180 tons of explosives. In total, almost 300 tons of explosives, over 1,000 bombs, fell on Ta' Qali, which was only approximately one-third of a square kilometre in size.

The situation on Malta was becoming desperate; military and civilian supplies were at their lowest. It was riskier than ever before to send supply convoys to Malta, especially from Gibraltar. But Britain needed to act to maintain control of the island. On 20 March, a large convoy, mostly formed of defensive ships and air cover, was sent from

Alexandria. When the convoy reached halfway between Alexandria and Malta, an offensive air strike was conducted on a North African air base to keep Axis air attacks at bay. However, the convoy was spotted and faced constant attack. Several vessels were sunk or destroyed; vessels that did make it into the Grand Harbour were also attacked and sunk after some supplies were unloaded; of the 25,000 tons sent, approximately 5,000 tons were unloaded and another 200 tons were able to be recovered from the sunken ships in the harbour.

For the Maltese people, the first few months of the year descended rapidly into the most intense period of the war to date. The island's offensive and defensive capabilities had been decimated, leaving the population exposed to further destruction. Any attempt to replenish the island was thwarted. The people were exhausted by the lengthy, late-night raids; many homes were destroyed and more families forced to live indefinitely underground in cramped, unpleasant conditions. The loss of civilian lives during the past two months had been devastating, more so than during any other period in the war. Food rationing was reduced even further, and it was estimated that fuel and kerosene would only last till June. Malta would experience its worst period of obliteration during a forty-day bombardment spanning March and April. Axis aircraft were involved in over 11,500 sorties, dropping over 6,500 tons of explosives, about half of those on Valletta. This figure would represent over forty-three per cent of the total tons of bombs that fell on Malta by the end of the war.

Around the world, the Allied effort was failing and the Axis effort was gaining strength. The British were struggling to maintain their territories in other parts of the world. In the space of a couple of months from late December to mid-February, the British Empire lost Hong Kong, Malaya and Singapore to the Japanese. Japan further asserted their dominance by taking Burma and Dutch East Indies (now Indonesia), while launching a strike on northern Australia. The British supply vessels in the Atlantic were annihilated, millions of tons of supplies lost to Axis submarines; this starved British war efforts in Egypt and the Middle East. Rommel was advancing in eastern Libya, retaking Benghazi by late January and progressing to the Egyptian border. The Germans were gaining ground in Russia, some thirty kilometres from Moscow. In March, Hitler ordered the construction of the Atlantic Wall: a series of fortifications with weaponry along the western seacoasts of Norway, Denmark, Germany, Holland, Belgium and France all the way to the border of Spain. This was to deter Allied attacks on the western front. The Axis powers had global supremacy and were increasing in strength. The US commitment to fight with the British against the Axis powers could not have been timelier; however, they were yet to have an impact.

Il-MIRAKLU TAL-BOMBA
(The Bomb Miracle)

Journal entry: 9 April 1942

Number four! Another life-altering experience notched on the belt of my short life. Not yet twenty and all within a two-year period; I'm sure most people don't encounter this many in their whole lifetime. These defining moments have been carved into my memory, vivid recollections that will stay with me as long as I live. First, there was the shock of war's declaration; my youth departed that day and adulthood hurriedly ushered in. Then came a shattered heart; every breath I take will carry the ache of an ever-open wound. Third, the brutal reality of war – the lifeless hand etched on my mind. And today, just hours ago, I was seized by a grip of terror like nothing I've felt before, heightened by my concern for mother by my side and the flashing thought of father alone. A bone-chilling incident that still reverberates through my body, evident in my unsteady hand. I'm rattled, yet strangely in a positive way. For the first time in a long time, I feel alive, as though electricity pulsates throughout my being. I'm tired but do not want to sleep, starved but do not want to eat; the experience of what I just lived through is too overwhelming to comprehend. Unlike the first three life-defining moments, this one had a fortuitous, even providential air about it. Before now, my scepticism regarding any godly existence had solidified due to the perpetual horrors and sufferings of this war – how could there possibly be a

God? Then again, is it fair to blame God, because he chose to give humanity free will, for humanity then using their free will to cause such pain and suffering? I don't know … One thing that's becoming clearer as time goes by is that there is an abominable evil presence in the world.

Today was different to most other days. I was given a rare day off from working at Lascaris. I had forgotten what it's like not to be in war mode, even though I still thought about it; it's hard not to when the evidence of war is all around. It was nice to spend the day with mother, who was often neglected by our daily absences. She visits the Basilica in the afternoons when she can. I wouldn't normally accompany her but I did this time, more so to spend time with her than anything else. The church was filled with hundreds of people praying in the silence. However, it wasn't long till an air raid siren broke the serenity. A scramble ensued; some left hastily, others ran into the sacristy, but mother and I stayed with the majority, moving towards the perimeter, hugging the walls. The siren soon mixed with the aggressive buzz of air engines approaching above. They've been pummelling the airfields of late, determined to render them useless cratered fields of rubble. I assumed they were going to pass over us on their way to Ta' Qali, not too far from here. There was a scream of bombs released, singing with one accord. No matter how many times I hear that sound, it still sends a shiver through my bones. My ears have become proficient in the art of determining whereabouts the bombs will fall – due to the sheer level of bombardment over these short years. As the squeals grew louder, so did my angst. My throat choked up and my eyes welled. I shouted, 'they're right above us!' There was a collective gasp and an increasing sense of alarm; we looked around at each other, looking for anyone to take the lead, but it was too late to run. The loudest boom I've ever heard, the closest I've been to a bomb above ground, just metres away! In the second before I closed my eyes, at the moment of impact, I saw the building shake and everyone drop to the floor. It sounded like the large unsupported dome was going to crash down on us, crushing us where we lay. There was another deafening thud of metal on masonry. I felt the rotunda wall violently shake; I leaned close against the wall while keeping my hand on mother's leg. Then a third thud in quick succession, a high-pitched screech, metal on marble. It was only seconds yet felt like minutes. Eyes still strenuously closed as I waited for the crash of the ceiling or the boom of the explosion, my heart beating out of my chest; the expectant moments were torture. All I could hear was the crumbing of debris falling from the ceiling and the sounds of explosions in the distance. After some seconds passed, I tentatively opened my eyes and lifted my head from the ground. I shook mother's leg, she looked back at me, both nodding to confirm we were okay. A white dust cloud hovered above the pews, the candle light still alive, flickering across the way through the haze. Large stones had crushed the pews where we had been moments before. I couldn't see the bomb but it was somewhere amongst us. A shout came from the other side of the Basilica, 'is everyone okay?' Everyone was fine – not a single scratch on anyone! The priest made haste and marshalled everyone away from the bomb into the sacristy. While waiting for the all-clear, mother and I held each other tightly; everyone was silent, many in deep prayer or reflecting on what had just occurred. I'm sure, like me, they sensed the unsettling tremble of a close call, pondering, 'how did I survive that?'

The explosive specialists quickly arrived on the scene to disarm the bomb. The congregation moved outside the Basilica, confiding in each other their shared experiences of a near life-ending moment, waiting for a glimpse of the bomb being taken away. I had an itch to see what had happened inside, to paint a picture of the sounds I had heard. I had been unable to make out what had happened through the cloudy haze and all-consuming haste of escaping the space. I slipped away and snuck in through the back unnoticed. I could hear the specialists discussing the best way to remove the bomb. The haze had settled, I looked up and I saw the blue sky through a hole in the ceiling large enough a small car could drive through. A ray of sunlight pierced through, illuminating the lingering fine dust particles drifting down. That must have been the initial hit, the deafening sound of which still echoed in my mind. I scoured the top of the wall and noticed damage to the corner of one of the frescoes depicting Jesus Christ with his disciples – this would have been the second thud that violently shook the walls. And there it was! This vicious weapon built for destruction, resting peacefully in this sanctuary on the scuffed and cracked marble floor. I looked up above where the bomb had settled. Amazingly, the bomb lay passive beneath the 'twelfth station of the cross' fresco, the one portraying Jesus dying on the cross to save humanity. Pondering what had just occurred, the thought of history repeating came to mind – I thought maybe Jesus again intervened to save those who were in the Basilica.

It was a reflective walk home for mother and I. We only spoke briefly about what had happened; she had been told that two smaller bombs fell on the Basilica grounds. One fell in the back in the yard and another hit the bell tower out the front – neither exploding! I thought it was amazing enough that one bomb didn't detonate, but three – all in a close vicinity – it's beyond belief!

The last two months have been the most devastating for the nation. With each passing day, our plight is only becoming worse and with it, the hopes of the nation deteriorate. Yet, these extraordinary moments, which seem to occur at just the right time, lift the nation and enliven our hope once again. Today's event was a phenomenal moment that will be engraved into Maltese history. I have no doubt that by this time tomorrow, the whole island would have heard about this miraculous occurrence. In fact, mother told me the people have already labelled the moment 'Il-Miraklu tal-Bomba'. It's difficult to disagree …

RS

Narrative: April–May 1942

On the first day of April, Kesselring continued his merciless bombardment, sending a fleet of almost 150 aircraft to attack Malta. The objective: to decimate the island's military capabilities and create an opportunity for Axis invasion. Constant air attacks by day to disrupt maintenance crew efforts to repair equipment and facilities; and by night, to disrupt and deprive the population of proper rest, especially the military. For several days, the island was defended by no more than one aircraft: and some days, none. The only remaining form of effective defence was the anti-aircraft guns, but the gunners were overwhelmed by the sheer numbers they encountered, attacked by 200, sometimes 300 aircraft in just one day.

On 7 April, Malta would endure the 2,000th air raid siren. The day also saw the worst attack on Valletta to date. Over 270 bombers attacked; the Royal Opera House was directly hit by Luftwaffe bombers, destroying the cherished building. Built in 1866, the building was an iconic piece of architecture, much admired by the people for its beauty and prominence in the capital. It is the only landmark not to have been rebuilt; today, the skeletal remains of the Royal Opera House stand as a testament and symbol of the Maltese resilience and operate as an open-air theatre.

In the small town of Mosta stands another of Malta's revered buildings. The Santwarju Bażilika ta' Santa Marija was built between 1833 and 1860. Situated near the Ta' Qali air base, approximately two kilometres away. The town had inadvertently endured heavy bombardment for months as it was in the direct flight path towards the noted Axis target, Ta' Qali airfield. An extraordinary event occurred at 4:40pm on 9 April. In the Basilica, around 300 people had gathered for evening prayer when an air raid sounded. Some ran for shelter, and others chose to stay. A 500-kilogram Luftwaffe bomb crashed through the dome ceiling, hitting an internal wall, then bouncing and skidding onto the ground. However, it did not explode; neither was anyone injured. Two smaller bombs fell nearby; one hit a corner of the bell tower and another bounced off the exterior dome and was found out back the Basilica; neither of these two bombs exploded. Finally, bomb disposal officers arrived to diffuse the explosives and remove the bombs from the Basilica grounds.

On 15 April, the King of England awarded the George Cross Medal to the nation of Malta and its people. This was an unprecedented gesture, since the award was typically given to individuals. The announcement provided a morale boost for the people and caught the attention of the Allied world. Congratulatory praise flooded in, reminding the people and military on the island that, although physically isolated, they indeed had the support of the Allied world. However, a handover ceremony would not take place until later in the year when it was safer to do so.

Malta was in grave danger of capitulating; supplying the island became near impossible; even the carpet runs were under threat. While one submarine was being unloaded, it was hit in an air attack and sunk. To make matters worse, the Axis continued to lay sea mines around the entry to the Grand Harbour. The island needed significant replenishment of aircraft. Churchill knew that the best way to defend Malta was to increase its air strike capabilities. However, the only way to obtain large shipments of aircraft was via aircraft carriers. He appealed to Roosevelt for the use of USS *Wasp*, a carrier that could fit over eighty aircraft, already in European waters. In late April, forty-seven Spitfires launched from the carrier and landed in Malta without interruption. However, in a devastating blow, forty of these were damaged on the ground in an air raid attack. A significant lesson was learned – to ensure that newly arrived aircraft were firing and ready to go. Further attempts were made in May, two separate deliveries totalling seventy-seven fighters, mostly Spitfires, were sent via USS *Wasp* and HMS *Eagle*, reaching the island safely and ready for immediate use. Shortly after receiving the first delivery, a fierce air battle ensued. The RAF pilots, coupled with the accuracy of the anti-aircraft gunners on the ground, destroyed over sixty enemy aircraft compared to a loss of only two Spitfires. In a week, almost 140 Axis aircraft had been destroyed.

One pilot of note was Canadian fighter pilot, George 'Buzz' Beurling. He was one of the greatest Allied pilots of the Second Word War. A man in his early twenties, he arrived on Malta in June. Assured in his ability, he fired only when he was confident he could hit the target, and he did so with great precision. Not one to shy away even when outnumbered, he chased enemy aircraft until he hit his target. In one incident on 8 August, several Luftwaffe aircraft were approaching the Grand Harbour. Beurling was on their tail; he successfully shot one down; however, his aircraft engine was hit by another fighter. Attempts to restart the engine failed, and he fell from the sky at speed. He was above Malta and prepared for as smooth a landing as possible. The problem was that the fields and paddocks of Malta were riddled with stone walls, making it incredibly difficult to find a stretch of open land. His plane went down in a field between Gudja Village and Tarxien; he successfully landed and managed to avoid the stone walls by mere centimetres. He exited the plane with only a scratch on his arm. By the end of his Malta campaign, Beurling had taken down twenty-seven confirmed Axis aircraft in fourteen flying days in the space of a three-month period: by far, the highest of any pilot defending Malta. He was awarded the distinguished Flying Cross for his outstanding piloting skills.

Despite the Maltese successes in the air, Kesselring was satisfied that he had destroyed Malta's effectiveness as an offensive Allied base. Most of the Axis convoys between Italy and North Africa were able to reach port. In April, over ninety per cent of Axis ships reached their destination. He advised Hitler that Malta had been nullified and Axis supply lines had been secured in the Mediterranean – that the island had been isolated from the outside world. Kesselring was resolute to proceed with plans for a land invasion, but Hitler had second thoughts. Content that the island had finally been neutralised, he chose to postpone the invasion of Malta for several months and focus on the Axis forces' advances in North Africa, into Egypt, and further into Russia. Kesselring was not happy – standing by his word that Malta must be taken for Axis victory in the region – but was somewhat mollified that the plan was not altogether rejected. Sicilian-based Luftwaffe units were relocated to bolster Axis campaigns in Russia and North Africa. A small contingent of Luftwaffe aircraft remained to ensure Malta remained subdued. Needless to say, this was a favourable outcome for Malta as the air attacks decreased in number and intensity.

The six months from November to April comprised the most attack-heavy period of the war for the Maltese. There was just one twenty-four-hour period in which the island was free of air raids. The people endured a period of 154 consecutive days and nights of bombardment. To put that into perspective, London – five times the size of Malta – endured a successive bombing period of only fifty-seven days. This level of aerial bombardment is the most concentrated and sustained air attack in world war history. Within the first two weeks of April, nearly 2,400 sorties flew over Malta, dropping over 3,000 tons of explosives, causing 340 casualties. The increased intensity of the fight was evident, with over 160,000 rounds fired from anti-aircraft guns in April compared to the 30,000 rounds in January. Everything that could be bombed had been, except the Grandmaster's Palace in Valletta, completed in the 18th century, the residence of the Grandmaster of the Order of St. John. The Germans intended to use that building as their military base upon occupation of Malta. By the end of May, when the most severe pummelling had subsided, much of Malta formed a desolate landscape, a wasteland of rubble everywhere and lingering haze. The island had been thrust back to a time before modern convenience: electricity, communication, water, amenities all affected and hardly functioning. The port and docking area were destroyed and unusable for repair workers. The Grand Harbour was a cesspool of stale oil, submerged vessels and bodies; protruding twisted metal and debris littered the harbour shoreline. An oil depot had been destroyed with much of aviation fuel lost. Countless armament, aircraft and ships were destroyed. Almost 16,000 buildings were destroyed, almost all of them homes. Up to eighty per cent of Valletta was damaged, and accessibility made difficult by mounds of debris blocking streets. Many towns and villages suffered over fifty per cent destruction. The British Parliament acknowledged the bravery of the Maltese people in enduring such an immense pounding from the skies. The concentration of bombardment far surpassed the most intense attack on Britain during the war.

7. Bomb damage in Valletta: a heavily damaged street in Valletta, Malta. On the right, the cherished Opera House destroyed.

8. Mosta Basilica.

9. Mosta Dome from the inside. Considered the fourth-largest unsupported dome in the world (third in Europe); 2.7 metres shorter in diameter than the dome of St. Peter's Basilica in Rome.

HELP!

Journal entry: 8 July 1942

Are we living our last days of freedom? Are we breathing our last breaths of liberty? We're a nation pressed to the extreme limits of suffering, enduring the worst of living conditions; and the path ahead indicates there is worse to come … It's hard to imagine what that 'worse' would look like; we are already scraping our fingernails on the bottom and can descend no further. It's as though we are no longer living, but rather existing in an alien landscape devoid of life apart from its fading inhabitants. Every time I step above ground, I wonder, 'am I still in Malta?' A sorry site of brokenness and extinction; hardly a street or building exists in its original state. The island's natural vibrancy has been reduced to a dim heartbeat. A lingering powdery haze hovers above the whole island, the result of constant pulverisation. The fine dust finds its way into everything; an unwanted ingredient in each bite, like grit between the teeth; gripping to oozing sores and scratching the eyes; the particles ride on every inhaled breath, feeding lung infections.

Though the storm has eased, the rain continues, not so much to destroy anything – everything has already been bombed – but to remind us that they are still there and will not go away. We no longer fear the falling sky; this fear has been replaced by the dread of lack. The collective growls of the people's stomachs sound as loud as the bombings. We can evade the bombs by hiding underground, but we can't evade starvation, illness and disease. Rationing mandates have become increasingly stringent over time, to the point that every item available has a consumption restriction. The four basic necessities for human survival – water, food, clothing and shelter – have been pummelled or dwindle near depletion; we are living in the days of residual crumbs.

The island's staples of bread and potatoes are becoming but remnants. Various food scraps – one obvious inclusion is potato skin – are added to dough to extend the bread supply. Wood and oil are scarce commodities, even more so than food. Trees felled and furniture wood have been used up; the cooking fires will soon be quenched. The bleat of barnyard noises has long fallen silent; now that I think upon it, it's been months since I last saw a live animal – except hearing the rare tweets of birds, the only animal quick enough to escape the desperate lunging grasp of a human hand. The community kitchens provide some relief but it's never enough. A piece of paper scribbled with '3 pence' can buy a bowl of watered-down beige broth with floating bits of (what's meant to be but doesn't quite resemble) vegetables, a herring and a spoonful of fruit preserve for the day. What would normally sound unappetising becomes a grand feast in these demanding times – certainly, no one would pass it up. I vaguely recall the delectable enjoyment of a home-cooked meal followed by a sweet dessert. One comfort I particularly long for is the refreshing cleansing warmth of a bath with a fragrant bar of soap. I would literally give my next day's ration to experience that again. Alas, such comforts have become a mere fantasy.

Many still wear the same clothes they escaped in months ago. Clothing has become two sizes too big, men piercing extra holes in their belts to keep their trousers from slipping down their withering waists, tatty clothing patched up with whatever is available. Women fashion dresses from curtains and parachute material; old blankets turned into winter coats; cardboard placed inside shoes to cover the holes, old tyre pieces used to re-sole shoes, held together with string.

With no place to go, many have no choice but to dwell underground, where despair and hopelessness are amplified. A chorus of coughing and moans resounds like the whimper of helpless mammals. It's heartbreaking, seeing the plight of my people, their dishevelled state, gaunt figures haunting in appearance, bones bulging beneath pale skin. Malnourished children with matchstick limbs, grubby and barefoot, sapped of youthful exuberance. Sanitation is non-existent; wound coverings are washed and reused, increasing disease and infection, along with already untreated health conditions, creating a subterranean plague-ridden civilisation. Human dignity has been ravaged from our society, our situation reduced to a sordid subhuman reality. We've become scavengers, left to forage for life's basic necessities, hiding in dank and dark underground caves; it seems I'm describing the lives of rodents.

The mental torture magnifies the physical anguish when we are teased by the announcement of a nourishing convoy on the way – only for it to be turned back, postponed or decimated on the journey. The enemy's attacks on supply convoys have been vicious, determined as they are to keep Malta isolated and to extinguish any attempt at life-sustaining provisions from reaching our shores. They are succeeding – our island is well and truly cut off from the outside world! Their stranglehold is tightening day by day and we're on the precipice of that fatal grasping clench that will cut the life off from the island; the blow that they think would drop us to our knees in begging surrender. It seems the enemy have got us where they want us; helpless in the palm of their hands, ripe for them to clamp down and devour us once and for all. Such thoughts should lead to a hopeless conclusion but, just like this island nation is built on a foundation of solid rock, the inner strength of the Maltese people is as granite. I've observed desperate need, and the appearance of my people wilt into emaciation; but, amazingly, I have seen their resilience increase through these ongoing hardships. The beating heart of the nation inspires me, hard pressed on every side, but not crushed, overwhelmed yet not giving in; suffocated, yet we fight on, struck down but not destroyed. Their attempt to starve us into submission is working in part. To starve us, yes. To make us submit, NO! We are still breathing, albeit faintly, but so long as we are breathing, we will not surrender; we will remain and withstand their harshest aggression rather than surrender to the governance of the despised Germans. If they come, we will not run.

We will fight in our streets, we will fight in our fields, we will fight for our country till the very end. It will be they – the enemy invaders – that will scream, 'Help!'

RS

Narrative: June–July 1942

The Axis plan to isolate the island was working; the lack of overall provisions, especially food and medical supplies, plunged the population into ever more deplorable living conditions. Such lack led to a greater threat of rampant disease, namely typhoid and polio, which were previously relatively unknown on the island. Military supplies were also in high demand, particularly fuel and ammunition. However, the departure of Luftwaffe fleets for other battles was timely, and the nation was able to conserve what remained of their military stock. The number of sorties flown over Malta had dropped substantially, from about 9,000 in April to 1,000 in June. However, Axis aircraft maintained constant patrols over Malta and were unyielding in their attempts to disrupt convoy supplies being sent to the island. However, there were no disruptions to aircraft resupply; another sixty Spitfires arrived on the island within the first two weeks of June. The arrival of the aircraft boosted Malta's ailing fleet; however, such aircraft would be useless without a continuing supply of fuel. It was estimated that current supplies would be exhausted by the end of August. The Maltese Command made a desperate call to Britain, asserting that without such supplies, the island would surely fall. Churchill heeded the call; he was resolute not to let Malta fall into the hands of the enemy.

Malta had not received a substantial supply convoy for several months. Large convoy attempts were made in June and July, but Axis assaults were intense, and many ships were destroyed or turned back. Surviving ships that endured the worst bombardment still had to navigate sea mines; in some instances, these sunk or damaged the vessels. In the largest attempt in June, two separate convoy operations from Gibraltar and Alexandria made their way to Malta simultaneously. A convoy from the eastern Mediterranean consisted of eleven merchant ships flanked by over forty defensive vessels. From the western Mediterranean came six merchant vessels containing nearly 45,000 tons of cargo, including the American oil tanker *Kentucky*, carrying a large supply of fuel and kerosene, covered by up to thirty defensive vessels at various points in the journey. The convoys came under immediate attack. The eastern convoy sailed from Haifa Port in Palestine and Port Said in Egypt. Following four days of attacks, of the eleven merchant ships, only five remained afloat. Due to constant pursuit by air units and the Italian Navy, fuel and ammunition were nearly exhausted; it was deemed unsafe to continue, so the eastern convoy attempt was abandoned and the remaining vessels turned back to Alexandria. The western supply convoy also received a battering, several vessels damaged or destroyed including the loss of the valuable oil tanker *Kentucky*. Of the six, two merchant ships, with approximately 15,000 tons of cargo, made it to Malta. In the first seven months of 1942, only five merchant ships managed to reach Malta, none of those a fuel tanker, and two of the five were destroyed at port. It was becoming a near impossible task to supply Malta with the substantial supplies it needed to survive. The most recent supplies extended Malta's predicted longevity by several weeks but did nothing to truly alleviate the situation; further rationing restrictions – which were already at dangerously low levels, insufficient for survival – were implemented. The Commander of the island broadcast a message to the nation regarding the grim situation. However, he assured the people that more convoy attempts would be made at the next opportune moment. He entreated everybody to keep their faith in God Almighty, appealing to the intrinsic spiritual heart of the nation to maintain its hope. Indeed, it would take an almighty effort to save Malta from a seemingly inevitable and desperate outcome.

The postponed land invasion of Malta, codenamed Operation Herkules, was planned for June. It would involve multiple points of entry, comprising paratroopers, followed by a seaborne landing that would involve thousands of troops. Allied reconnaissance spotted a number of tank-landing craft amassing in Axis ports, signalling an imminent land invasion. The Maltese Command was prepared, increasing the number of anti-parachute battalions around the island. The Malta Volunteer Defence Force was created, primarily comprised of civilians; they were given firearms and placed in charge of guarding their towns. However, the invasion of Malta would once again be stalled; Rommel required more military equipment and personnel to maintain his advance in North Africa. Hitler sided with Rommel, to Kesselring's disdain, and Operation Herkules was postponed, once again, till mid-to-late August. Kesselring reiterated his stance that securing Malta was of utmost importance, highlighting that the very reason gains were being made in North Africa was because Malta had become less able to attack Axis supply lines. Rommel acknowledged that his success in North Africa was in part due to a subdued Malta and agreed with Kesselring that the island needed to be secured once and for all. Kesselring's concerns were valid; Malta kept fighting on and continued to pester the Axis powers, thwarting air attacks and continually disrupting their supply convoys, albeit only to a minor extent. The island's air force was increasing, with another fifty-nine Spitfires arriving in July. The absence of large Luftwaffe fleets meant that the RAF were on par in the skies, able to nearly match the number of Axis aircraft by sending up fifty Spitfires and Hurricanes at any one time. By the end of July, offensive strikes had steadily increased and bombing raids on Malta were at their lowest since the end of 1941.

Elsewhere, the British launched air raid attacks on the German cities of Essen, Bremen and Cologne; this would be the last major British bombing campaign until 1944. Rommel's forces swept through North Africa, taking Tobruk in June and entering Egypt by July, as well as beginning their attack on El Alamein, which lay 100 kilometres away from the main British military base in Alexandria. Japan secured a piece of US territory: the Attu and Aleutian Islands, part of Alaska. However, their goal of removing America from the Pacific took a hit when they lost the Battle of Midway. Japan had control of all of South-East Asia and half of Papua New Guinea, within striking distance of Australia. The Germans continued their advance into the USSR, now perched just outside Stalingrad and continuing southward into the Caucasus region. Hitler's gains in this region steeled his resolve to capture Egypt. His plan was to sweep downward from the USSR through the Caucasus region, while advancing northward through Egypt in a pincer-like move; this would surround the much-prized oil fields of the Middle East, currently in the hands of the Allies.

THE LAST HOPE

Journal entry: 9 August 1942

This is it! The last hope of a nation on the verge of capitulation. Over two years of continual struggle, bombardment and destruction. The military fight is fast losing steam; the people's threshold of suffering has been tested beyond its limits, an inch away from complete starvation – the only sustenance keeping us going of late is the last remnants of hope.

The daily four pages of the *Times of Malta* raise the confidence of the people, declaring a saviour convoy to come within days … if it does in fact reach us. Britain has prepared the largest ever convoy to be sent to Malta, giving us the best possible chance of merchant ships reaching us. Tomorrow, the liberating fleet will set sail, as though a trespasser entering a hornet's nest. Once the fleet sails out of Gibraltar's protective reach, however, it will drift into the shadows of the volatile and ravenous beast. What lies ahead of the floating vessels of hope is an Axis barrage of dogged annihilation – the ironclad Axis western Mediterranean curtain, kilometres thick, near impossible to pass through without enemy-inflicted scars. It will be absolute mayhem! I can't imagine what one would feel, about to enter such hostile territory. I'm in awe of the servicemen participating in the operation, risking their lives for the people of Malta so we can keep living in freedom – and for goodness to prevail over evil. No matter the outcome, these servicemen will be heroes of the nation. Every man, woman and child will be riding every moment of the convoy's perilous 2,000-kilometre journey, as though we are sailing with them.

I've never been more anxious in my life! In a few days, we will know the fate of the nation. Have we fought in vain? Have we withstood hardship for nothing? Or will there be vindication finally? It breaks my heart to think that we could surrender after everything we've resisted over the years. But I concede the reality of our plight; in the past week, more supplies have been completely exhausted: sugar and cooking oil. I understand why surrender is an option; soon there will be nothing; life must improve for the people's sake. But would it? We would live under the enemy's tyranny; no evidence suggests they possess compassion for humanity. We'd most likely be treated as chattel, devalued goods, pawns of war – I'm weakened by the thought! We can't end up like this. The convoy must reach us, it just must!

On this momentous eve of what will most certainly define the nation, we wait, we hope and we pray. It's become so clear that this nation rests on a bedrock of faith. The churches, even the partially standing ones, are full of people. In the underground shelters, there's a constant hum of prayer hanging in the air. Waiting in line at the communal kitchens, a mumble of grateful praise for what they are about to receive. Our faith is the one thing the enemy can't destroy or take from us. We may be lacking the necessities to sustain the physical but certainly not the spiritual. Prayer has become the staple of the Maltese spirit, uplifting the soul of the nation, and undoubtedly it is what has kept this nation going. I'm sure everyone, even those unsure of what they believe, will be sending up a prayer these next few days – I certainly will. The means to fight may be all but diminished, but the will to fight endures. We may not have the arms to overpower the mighty enemy, but as a nation we have the faith to move the arm of the Almighty, and that … is all the hope we need.

RS

Narrative: August 1942

Malta was on the brink of collapse; some food stores were mere days or weeks from completely running out, which would lead to nationwide starvation. The lack of fuel and ammunition had greatly reduced both offensive and defensive strikes, rendering the island inoperable as a military base. The situation was so dire that a secret surrender date was agreed upon by the Maltese Command: between mid and late September. Churchill remained adamant regarding the importance of Malta to the Empire; loss of the island would be detrimental to the Allied fight in the region and beyond. In Churchill's words, the loss of Malta would be 'a disaster of [the] first magnitude'. If Malta was lost, British ships in the Mediterranean would be forced to retreat, giving the Axis powers unfettered access to the region; the Afrika Korps would continue to strengthen and take the entire North African coastline including Egypt and, subsequently, the Middle East.

Despite the failure of previous convoy attempts in recent months, approval was given by the British Parliament for the largest merchant supply cargo and most heavily escorted Allied convoy ever assembled in the war, indeed, in warfare history at that point in time. It was codenamed Operation Pedestal. In July, the planning began, utilising a plethora of available ships from Britain, the Middle East and the USA. The success of the operation was critical to Malta's longevity as an effective Allied base. The island was running out of time, meaning this would be the last major convoy attempt to prevent imminent surrender.

The convoy comprised fourteen merchant ships carrying a combined supply tonnage of over 150,000. It would be flanked by sixty-five other vessels in the convoy procession: battleships, aircraft carriers, cruisers, destroyers, submarines and corvettes. Thirteen of the fourteen merchant vessels carried various food, medical and military provisions. The final merchant vessel needed to be an oil tanker: a large, fast oil tanker that could hold a huge consignment of fuel. Without such a tanker, the convoy would serve only to sustain the people but not the fight. Initially, it seemed that no such tanker was available; the British did not possess any that were reliable. The

Americans did have Navy oil tankers; however, these were needed for their fight in the Pacific. The search was expanded and a non-Navy oil tanker was found: an American oil tanker already in British waters, having just delivered its first fuel shipment to Britain. Churchill spoke with Roosevelt who agreed to lend the oil tanker to the vital operation: a tanker purposely built for the Texaco Oil Company named *Ohio*.

Ohio was the sister ship to *Kentucky*, which had met its demise in a supply operation to Malta in June. *Ohio* was built in 1940 and was the largest (over 9,200 tons and 155 metres long) and fastest (up to thirty kilometres per hour) oil tanker ever built at that point in time. It also had a greater fuel capacity than any tanker built previously; at full capacity, it could hold over 20,000 tons of fuel. The tanker was built like no other – the first of its kind. Specially designed and welded, containing many individual cargo tanks, and stronger than all other tankers; the *Ohio* was robustly built – indeed, it was the perfect vessel for such a perilous operation. However, it remained a non-military ship and was devoid of military capabilities. And so began a mad rush to modify the oil tanker with military defensive and other capabilities. The *Ohio* was fitted out in Glasgow: anti-aircraft guns mounted on decks, sides reinforced with steel plates to protect from torpedoes. To avoid the failures of past convoys, the interior was also strengthened: the engine mounted on a rubber base and critical piping was supported to minimise the shock from explosions. *Ohio* would be the most crucial vessel of the merchant fleet, carrying over 11,000 tons of fuel.

Intelligence gathered by Axis forces alerted them to a large Allied convoy on its way to Malta via the western Mediterranean. The Germans and Italians had already positioned over 1,200 aircraft – fighters, bombers, torpedo bombers, dive bombers and other aircraft – around the Mediterranean at Axis bases in Sicily, Sardinia, North Africa and Pantelleria. More than half were instantly available to engage with the vessels of Operation Pedestal. Also at the ready was the Italian naval fleet, ranked the fifth-largest in the world (larger than those of Germany and Russia), comprising six battleships, over eighty cruisers and destroyers, and over 100 submarines. The Axis objective was clear: to annihilate every single vessel of Operation

Pedestal. Malta-based attacks had long been a thorn in the side of Axis convoy supply routes – and they relished the opportunity for revenge.

Vessels involved in Operation Pedestal

Fourteen merchant ships: vessels designed to carry various supplies including ammunition, food, mechanical equipment and spares, medical supplies and various weaponry. *Ohio* carried the vast majority of fuel; all other merchant ships held small containers of fuel.

Two battleships: large war vessels over 200 metres long. Heavily armoured and laden with large guns and high explosives: the dominant vessel of the sea.

Four aircraft carriers: large vessels that acted as an airbase on the sea. Over 200 metres in length, primarily used to carry aircraft to destinations. One aircraft carrier accompanied the convoy for a special operation to launch aircraft to Malta and turned back when the operation was complete after two days of sailing.

Seven cruisers: a smaller version of a battleship, fast vessels equipped with high-powered guns, approximately 150–180 metres in length.

Eight submarines: underwater vessels that operated clandestinely, equipped with missiles to attack encroaching Axis vessels.

Thirty-two destroyers: high-speed vessels equipped with guns, torpedoes and anti-submarine weapons, 80–120 metres in length.

Four minesweepers: small vessels that clear the waterways of sea mines by detonating or removing the explosives so that Allied vessels could pass through unhindered.

Two tugs: the mules of the sea, small robust vessels that helped guide ships through tight waterways or pushed them along if they were unable to move under their own steam.

Two oilers: large ships that carried fuel for the vessels partaking in the convoy operation, ensuring that the vessels were well fuelled for the journey that would take days.

Four corvettes: small warships specifically designed for anti-submarine warfare, equipped with guns and depth charges.

The Axis war machine was at the height of its powers in the region and mainland Europe, the air and sea infested by its presence. Operation Pedestal seemed an irrational mission, one that would most likely end in utter obliteration; however, it was one of the most crucial endeavours of the Second World War. For most of the journey, there would be no outside protection for the convoy until it reached the air cover provided by Malta.

Already, Malta had withstood the most aggressive and violent air attacks in warfare history; now, over the next few days, the people would need to endure such anxious moments, which would ultimately determine the fate of the nation. Operation Pedestal would embark from the western Mediterranean on 10 August and would endure an unprecedented barrage of enemy fire not seen on the Mediterranean seas in all of history.

10. Ohio tanker before being fitted for Operation Pedestal.

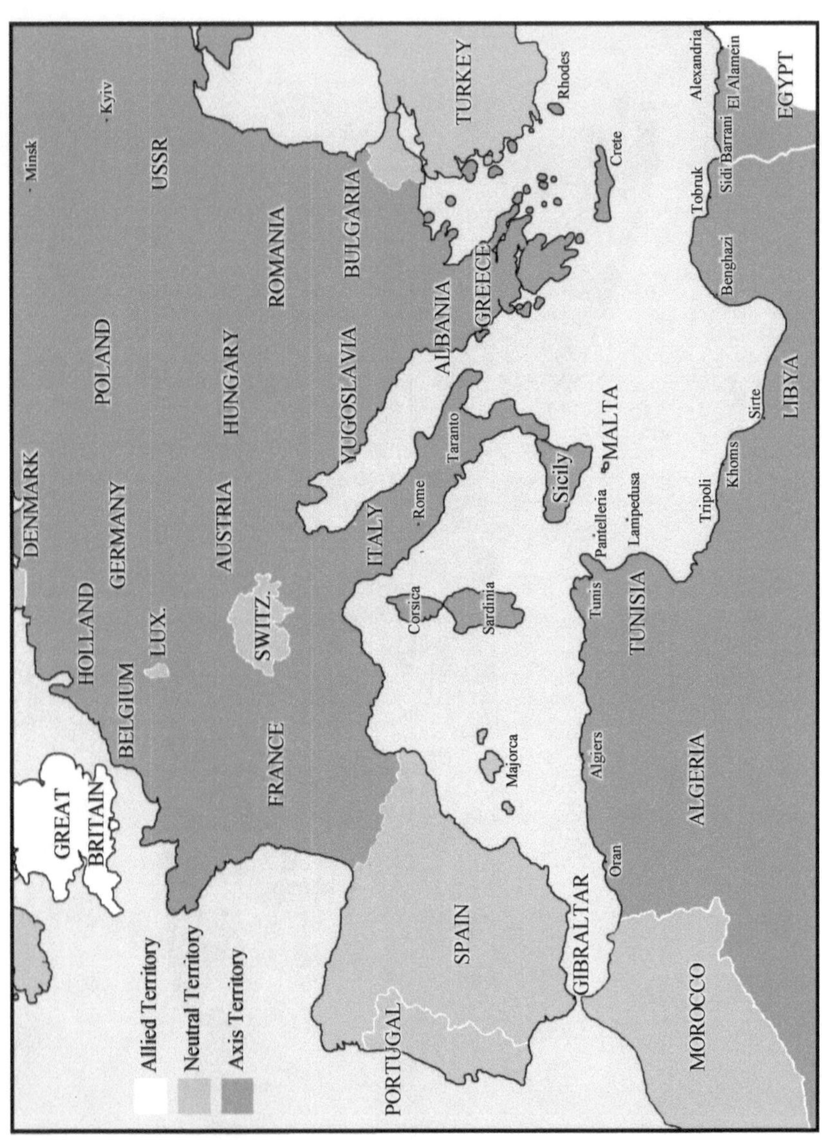

11. European map of control; mid-1942. Map shows Malta completely isolated: Gibraltar and Egypt the closest Allied support. The Axis area includes the puppet territories.

ENGULFED

Journal entry: 13 August 1942

The resting rooms at Lascaris are anything but restful; who can rest in agonising anticipation? I can't go home, not because I'm not allowed – I don't want to. The gripping need to know what's happening, as it happens, is consuming me. Proper sleep is evasive; the physical part of me shuts down while my mind remains alert to the distant chaotic chatter and clatter of the main command room. The slightest increase in sound and I instantly leap up with a racing heartbeat. I hurriedly check on the latest updates; anxiously, I loiter the periphery, glued to the walls so as not to get in anyone's way – shoulder to shoulder with other anxious observers – nibbling my fingernails, desperately awaiting the next morsel of news. The mayhem subsides in the deep night hours, many worn out by the day's events. The senior commanders, including father, hardly have proper respite. We're in close proximity, yet I haven't spoken to him in three days. He's intensely invested in the success of the current operation and I don't want to disturb him.

As this day was coming to its end, it seemed the nation was panting its last breaths. Since the convoys disembarked till this morning, the news had been dire, teetering on the cusp of hopelessness: merchant ship after merchant ship sunk, the hopes of the nation sinking with them. Making matters ever more nerve-racking is that communication lines have been severed; we're unsure of real-time events out at sea, reliant upon reconnaissance updates. The outcome has appeared to be fruitless; I've been resigned to the complete annihilation of the nation's last hope. But then … a spark of elation ignited in the growing gloom; loud cheers and applause reverberated throughout Lascaris. Three merchant vessels were spotted approaching in the distance; I raced to the upper harbour to watch them sail into port. A Godsend for our deprived nation, our first substantial provision in months, which we so desperately needed. It was a bittersweet moment, however; I was grateful for the arrival of the three supply ships, considering nine others had been destroyed. Yet, two more vessels remained on the perilous open seas, and the merchant ship this nation needs most is one of these.

The jubilation is short lived; attention turns to Ohio, which is still afloat – although, by all reports, barely. The hunter returns again and again to the maimed prey, determined to land the decisive blow. Amazingly, Ohio remains alive – and with it, the nation's hope. The intense bombardment has shifted from the land to the sea. I'd rather they bombed the island than the remaining convoy; that's how much we need it! Since the beginning of the operation, Father has said repeatedly, 'Ohio must make it!' All the commanders agree; it's a near miracle that Ohio is still afloat. The precious fuel cargo is the lifeblood for our nation's continued fight.

It's a daunting predicament, the vulnerable vessel will remain perhaps two more days on the volatile seas, a sitting duck open to incessant harassment from Axis-laden seas and sky. The situation screams impossible; the odds are heavily against Ohio basking in the light of another day in the Mediterranean sun. It's not even running on its own steam … it drifts precariously and is slowly sinking; it seems inevitable that Axis bombers will pick it off – a much larger target than the other nine merchant vessels. I wrestle with angst about a possibly ominous conclusion. But I retain the slightest morsel of hope due to the collective faith of the nation. During my times on the upper harbour, I gaze upon the anticipating crowd, eyes closed in serenity, hands clasped against their chests, lips moving inaudibly; this nation has never lost hope, has never abandoned faith, despite the overwhelming circumstances. This nation once again prays in wait.

Indeed, we've experienced some miraculous turns of events just when all had seemed lost; perhaps it's the engulfing prayers of the nation that are keeping Ohio afloat …

RS

Narrative: August 1942

On the 10th, Operation Pedestal sailed into the western Mediterranean, which was enemy controlled and heavily monitored. Over 20,000 personnel would take part in the operation. The journey was over 2,000 kilometres long; vessels were spaced approximately 500 metres apart. Air defence cover was at the ready: accompanying carriers *Eagle*, *Indomitable* and *Victorious*, carrying over seventy fighters between them. A fourth aircraft carrier, *Furious*, was in tow, assigned with the sole directive to launch Spitfires to Malta. Simultaneously, two smaller convoys, complete with defensive escorts, sailed from the eastern Mediterranean, Port Said and Haifa: a diversionary tactic to deflect attention and Axis resources from the main convoy. However, it failed to achieve the desired effect, due to discovered intelligence; the Axis knew that the western convoy was the vital supply run.

The first day was uneventful, like a peaceful summer cruise on the Mediterranean. After midday on the 11th, the operation to send Spitfires from *Furious* began as the convoy approached the wider seas above Algiers, which were infested with Axis submarines. RAF pilots took off from *Furious*, but when they steadied in the air, they looked down in dismay; they could see torpedo trails in close proximity to the convoy – and there was no time to send a warning. Just after 1 pm, directly south of Majorca, the aircraft carrier *Eagle* suffered the first strike; it was hit by four submarine torpedoes. This was a destructive blow; personnel from the surrounding vessels watched on in horror as the large carrier tipped on its side and sunk in just seven minutes. This effectively took out one-third of the convoy's air power, limiting the number of planes that could be in the air at any one time. The loss of such a key vessel so early was devastating; of the 1,087 crew members, 160 lost their lives and only four of the twenty planes were able to fly off. The attack paused the operation to launch Spitfires from *Furious* until the aircraft carrier had navigated to a safer position. By 2:30 pm, all thirty-six Spitfires had launched, landing safely in Malta; with its mission complete, *Furious* turned back to Gibraltar, escorted by eight destroyers.

By evening, the convoy had reached the halfway point of its journey; and just before 9 pm, the first air attack occurred. However, the ships' anti-aircraft gunners and RAF fighters were able to deter the enemy, and the convoy continued on its journey throughout the night relatively unscathed.

As the convoy progressed, the danger increased. On the morning of the 12th, the convoy approached the stretch of waters beneath the Cagliari Axis air base in Southern Sardinia. In the dawn hours, Axis reconnaissance flights could be seen overhead; it was only a matter of time before waves of air bombardment followed. The first air attack of the day occurred just after 9 am, coupled with attacks from the sea. There were several clashes throughout the day; each air battle was an aerial dogfight, a deafening chaos of whistling and exploding bombs, constant gunfire and a swarm of screaming aircraft. The convoy's air fleet were considerably outnumbered, as much as 100 against just twenty. When the attacks subsided by 10 pm, the convoy was in disarray; three merchant ships, one cruiser and one destroyer had been sunk. The aircraft carrier *Indomitable*, two cruisers and a destroyer had been damaged. The destroyer was damaged when it rammed into a surfaced Axis submarine – effectively sinking it – when the convoy came upon a group of Italian submarines lying in wait; the other submarines were chased away by the destroyer's depth charges. Another two merchant ships were struck, damaged and then strayed away from the main convoy group; one drifted north but sunk later that night. The other merchant vessel, the *Brisbane Star*, was hit by a torpedo that created a huge hole in the bow and began taking on water; it could not maintain pace and veered south, also losing touch with the main convoy. The sunken cruiser, *Cairo*, and one of the damaged cruisers, *Nigeria*, were the only two vessels fitted with long-range radar and high-powered communications; thus, the convoy lost its ability to communicate with Command Headquarters on Malta. The aircraft on the damaged *Indomitable* were diverted to *Victorious*, now the only operational carrier. The preserved vessels steamed ahead while damaged vessels returned to Gibraltar, with the exception of *Ohio* – damaged by a torpedo strike, it had fallen behind the main group of ships. The strike tore an eight-metre hole in the side, igniting some of its cargo, which created an upward explosion and destroyed a large part of the upper deck. A fire raged dangerously close to the kerosene tank; it was feared the whole tanker would explode. The hit had damaged the main steering and compass instruments and a large metal plate now stuck out from its side, which made the tanker veer in circles. The captain gave orders to shut down the engines to stop *Ohio* drifting, and to douse the flames. One might think an eight-metre hole in a ship's side could serve no purpose; however, the water gushing in greatly helped to subdue the fire; the flames were eventually contained and *Ohio* was able to begin moving again. The rudder was fixed to one side to counter the drag from the protruding metal plate, while the destroyer *Ledbury* aided the compass-less tanker through the darkness by sailing ahead with a light to guide the way.

That evening, the convoy had passed beneath Sardinia and was heading towards the most hazardous stretch of the journey, the Sicilian Narrows. The Sicilian Narrows lie between Sicily and the Tunisian prong of Cap Bon. The lands curve towards one another, narrowing to a width of just 145 kilometres. To make matters more perilous, a large minefield lay in the middle of the stretch. The only way around was either between the minefield and Sicily, or between the minefield and Tunisa. Both were risky endeavours, practically delivering the convoy to within a few kilometres of the doorstep of Axis air bases. It became a choice of the lesser of two evils; the convoy would take the southerly option, via the coast of Tunisia.

As darkness set in, a large contingent of defensive vessels turned back to Gibraltar; twenty-six vessels returned, including the two battleships and the remaining aircraft carrier. This was due to the narrower waters, which would have exposed the vessels, especially the larger ones. The departure of the carrier left the fleet at its most vulnerable, without proper air defence and yet to enter the range of protective RAF fighters based on Malta. The remaining vessels moved to a two-column formation; the reduced convoy escorting the merchant vessels comprised four cruisers, twelve destroyers and four minesweepers.

After midnight on the 13th, the leading convoy was still over 400 kilometres from Malta, and the straggling *Ohio* was thirty kilometres behind them. However, *Ohio*'s lag proved fortunate; from 1 am, the main convoy ahead endured a merciless barrage from Axis aircraft, torpedo boats and submarines for four hours. Many vessels were damaged; among those that sunk before the light of day were four merchant ships and a cruiser. By morning, *Ohio* had caught up and was close behind the leading group of ships. Half the merchant vessels had made it through the Sicilian Narrows, but the danger was far from over as the convoy entered the range of surrounding Luftwaffe fleets.

The convoy was now within the protection of long-range fighters on Malta; however, damage to the convoy's communication lines meant that their exact location was unknown. Aircraft had to search for the convoy in order to provide sufficient air cover. Just after 8 am, waves of Luftwaffe bombers engaged the convoy. One merchant ship, carrying fuel and ammunition, exploded due to a direct hit. The explosion was so intense that a pursuing enemy aircraft was consumed by the upward fire blast, and minor damage was caused to another merchant ship one kilometre away.

The air attacks became concentrated on *Ohio*, distinguishable from the air by its larger size. In one instance, twenty-six Axis bombers launched an all-out assault on the tanker. Gunners on *Ohio* and a nearby destroyer erratically launched an upward hail of flak: projectiles that exploded in the air and released metal fragments that would tear through aircraft. The sheer number of enemy aircraft was overwhelming; fighters and dive bombers were coming from every direction and aircraft that were shot down would veer towards the tanker in the attempt to dive-bomb *Ohio*. One of the Axis fighters was shot down, ricocheted off the water, and crash-landed on *Ohio*'s foredeck. Another downed aircraft crash-landed onto the rear deck, narrowly avoiding the fuel below, separated by only five centimetres of steel. After 10 am, another air attack targeted *Ohio*; several near misses rattled the tanker, buckling and cracking the ship's plates, resulting in it taking on yet more water. Two nearby explosions, either side of the tanker, lifted the tanker – it came back down with a violent jolt, further unsettling the already ailing vessel. The near misses had destroyed the rudder and disabled the engines; frantic attempts were made throughout the morning to get the tanker going, its speed reduced to a slow drift. Just before midday, an explosion in the engine room would completely take out the ship's propulsion – the engines had stopped for good.

Again, *Ohio* lost pace with the group of vessels. A mess riddled with cracks, fractures and holes, an awkwardly heavy floating container of fuel and oil made all the more heavier by the tons of seawater it had taken on, it was reliant upon smaller vessels to drag it along. One destroyer, *Penn*, remained to assist, connecting a twenty-five-centimetre-wide towing rope; however, due to the ship's weight and propensity to veer to one side – due to the protruding metal plate – the towing line came apart. Other vessels were needed to assist the towing effort; until such time, *Ohio* was a sitting target. The captain made a call to disembark *Ohio*'s crew; it was widely believed that the tanker would inevitably sink. By 2 pm, *Ohio*'s crew crammed onto *Penn*. The destroyer remained nearby as cover for the tanker while remaining afloat. Over three hours later, as another vessel arrived, *Ohio*, although sinking lower into the sea, remained buoyant. *Ohio*'s crew reboarded and the supporting vessel, minesweeper *Rye*, began to tow the estimated 30,000-plus-ton deadweight to Malta. The group of ships, connected by cables, made little progress and would endure a rough night. Axis raids came in waves from 6:30 pm onwards. Axis bombers were met by Malta's Spitfires. Fierce air battles ensued. The anti-aircraft gunners and Spitfires did well to engage the bombers; however, some succeeded in sneaking past their defence and unleashing their loads. One bomb crashed through the upper foredeck and exploded within the tanker. Remarkably, it missed the flammable fuel and oil tanks, detonating in the engine room, causing major flooding. The captain of *Penn* broke the towline, deeming it too dangerous to be in the vicinity of *Ohio*, given that *Penn* was carrying survivors from other sunken vessels. Another destroyer, *Bramham*, arrived to assist with towing efforts; but by that night, after several waves of attacks, all cables to *Ohio* had been severed. *Ohio* once again became a motionless target and its crew disembarked yet again. All accompanying ships would remain with *Ohio*, as if holding a vigil; they were certain the tanker would break up and go under. However, long after the Axis attacks had ended for the night, *Ohio* remained afloat. Though *Ohio* was unmanned, towing efforts resumed. Cables were attached to the tanker, pulling her along at only seven kilometres an hour. During the hours ahead, the towlines would snap twice. The sheet of metal protruding from the tanker's side, along with the vessel's dragging buoyancy, made it increasingly difficult to keep the large tanker moving straight ahead. Having to work in the darkness also made matters more difficult; personnel wished to avoid turning lights on and alerting their enemies lurking beneath the sea. The situation looked hopeless as daylight was approaching; the dawning of the sun would bring with it more Axis attacks.

Earlier that evening, however, just after 6 pm, the first merchant vessel arrived into the Grand Harbour, followed shortly by two more merchant vessels. Thousands of volunteers were at the ready to unload the cargo. However, the most important vessel of the convoy remained stranded out at sea. The freedom and continued fight of Malta depended on the fuel contained on *Ohio*, and thus on the ship reaching its destination; the operation would not be a success otherwise.

12. Operation Pedestal: The operation begins. An aerial view of some of the ships escorting the convoy. In the forefront: aircraft carriers HMS Eagle, HMS Indomitable and HMS Victorious.

13. Operation Pedestal: The tanker Ohio under heavy attack.

14. Operation Pedestal: Sailors watch HMS Eagle sinking after being torpedoed

OHIO MIRACLE

Journal entry: 15 August 1942

I woke this morning in a sudden burst. In that initial waking moment, it had escaped me, but the uncomfortable confines of the resting room soon reminded me why I was there. Today was the day! Would Ohio enter the reaching arms of the harbour to nestle in her welcoming embrace? I hurried to the upper bastions; it was eerily silent in those last remnants of darkness before the first light of dawn, yet many were already waiting in hope. Ironically, I wanted to hear the guns and planes because that would mean Ohio was still there and fighting on. I approached Mr Vella who had kept vigil all night. He said he had heard the faint sounds of planes, guns, bombs, then silence. He continued with tears in his eyes, 'I hope she's still afloat'.

The horizon line appeared in the soft glow of the emerging sun; more people packed the bastions and vantage points around Valletta and across the harbour at Senglea, Vittoriosa and Kalkara, anxiously awaiting the arrival of this one ship, the ship of ships we so desperately needed, more than any other ship during the war. The light increased on this uncertain new day; everyone's gazes fixated out upon the sea. The rising sun was to lift the dark veil to reveal if our nation's last hope had made it. Someone shouted across the way, 'look!' It reverberated around the harbour and the background murmur fell to a hush. I squinted, scanning the yet-to-be-illuminated portion of the horizon. I couldn't see it at first, but then, from the disguising darkness emerged what looked like a clump of vessels. As the light continued to grow, so did the throng of people, surging to any vantage point they could find. Onlookers on fortified walls and buildings; not an empty space remained. The crowd was several bodies deep; it seemed the whole nation was there. A hopeful chatter swept through the swelling crowd, uncertain of which vessels we could see in the shady distance – but one was long enough to be a tanker! The creeping sunlight revealed the vessels and the state of Ohio; the more exposure from the sun, the more the excited noise dimmed to an anxious silence. Something was terribly wrong. What was once a proud and robust tanker, which stood tall within the fleet, now barely recognisable. Half the height it should be; the deck had fallen into line with the sea, waves lapping the deck, flanked by smaller vessels dragging it along. The group of ships crept closer to the mouth of the harbour; it seemed Ohio would sink if it weren't for the supporting vessels on either side. I'm sure the thought crossed all our minds, 'would Ohio make it to port?' The sounds were disheartening; metal on rock emanated from beneath as the bottom of the tanker scraped the seabed. The groaning creaks and stressful shrieks of rubbing metal and straining cables echoed throughout the harbour, as though Ohio itself was screaming in pain.

The crowd was dreadfully silent, fearing the ill tanker would crumble at any moment, right there at the harbour mouth – so close, yet so far! The men took off their hats, clutching them closely to their chests; women made the sign of the cross. I muttered an anguished prayer, 'please God, bring Ohio to port'. An elderly lady next to me heard me; she was small in stature but exuded an aura of mightiness in her faith. Unlike most of us, she was calm and spoke with compelling confidence: 'it's going to make it darling'. She raised her withered hand, pointing towards the incoming vessels and continued, 'this is the saviour's fleet … look'. And there it was! My eyes welled at the incredible sight, the three ships side by side, with Ohio in the middle. The masts stood high, resembling the three crosses on Calvary. Right then, I sensed a moment of peace – perhaps everything was going to be okay. Then, the surreal reverie was broken by the deep sound of the tanker horn, blaring twice in quick succession. An elated individual in the distance couldn't contain his exuberance, repeating at the top of his voice, 'it's going to make it, it's going to make it!' His declaration resounded throughout the harbour. The crowd remained silent for a moment before an eruption of cheers and shouts of joy rose from all around the perimeter of the Grand Harbour – and what a grand moment it was! A sea of Maltese, British and American flags lifted high above the crowd, coupled with the waving of handkerchiefs and the flinging of hats tossed in the air. Many had their hands clasped in reverent gratitude; tears of joy filled the eyes of the weary while others jumped up and down in rejuvenated delight. Strangers hugged each other, there was dancing and singing. Children running around chanted, 'convoy, convoy!' A brass band appeared and began playing 'Rule Britannia'. An aircraft approached the Grand Harbour, one of ours. The fighter pilot flew his Spitfire low through the Grand Harbour, upside down; the crowd lifted with a raucous cheer at his acrobatics. It was an incredible scene, carnival-like. I couldn't contain my emotion, galloping like a gazelle through the elated crowd; I wanted to cherish the memory of being there when we received this precious cargo. Along the way, a handsome young man grabbed my hand and spun me around; gladly, I obliged. The docks were a scramble of activity, a frantic rush to unload the cargo while the ship was still buoyant. The sound of cracking and creaking became more intense as Ohio's cargo was exhumed. Finally, Ohio settled on the seabed with a thud and breathed its last. Onlookers were tearful at the sight. It seemed as though the tanker had known it must accomplish its destiny, and could not give up until the life-saving cargo was delivered. From what I've witnessed today, it's not hard to believe the tanker was held together by divine hands.

Today's events encompassed the limits of our emotions, the depressing lows to the ecstatic highs. The day began with the nation's hope consumed by the still darkness. The sun was going to rise on a different Malta – one way or another. Ohio entered the Grand Harbour with the rising sun; they accompanied one another and delivered a new hope for the nation. It seemed the ailing tanker inched forward by the increasing strength of the sun: a new dawn rising over Malta. With it, a new sense of hope swept throughout the hearts of the people. As the sun rose, so did the hopes of the nation. Undoubtedly, today's sunrise will be the most glorious – miraculous even – sunrise the nation has ever seen. What we had feared would be the nation's darkest hour was revealed instead to be the nation's most magnificent, brightest hour. The people have been revived and so has our fight! Now more than ever, the resilience to hold firm is fierce. The jubilation I experienced today was unlike anything I've seen – or surely will ever see – on this island. A moment that will undoubtedly be engraved in Maltese history as one of its greatest moments.

RS

Narrative: August 1942

In the early hours of the 14th, *Ohio* lay motionless in the water, less than 100 kilometres from Malta. The destroyer, *Ledbury*, had rejoined the supporting vessels to assist in the rescue; several attempts were made to tow *Ohio* along, but to no avail; the thick cable kept coming undone. There was a sense of resignation, that nothing could be done to rescue the ailing tanker; but the crew were not going to abandon the vessel as long as it remained afloat. That morning, the captain reboarded *Ohio* to assess the damage. The deck was torn up and had collapsed in sections; the ship was buckled, her back broken, hull near bursting point, engine room destroyed; the fuel pumps, steering, rudder and compass were damaged and not functioning – the whole ship completely out of power. The bow was pointing upwards. Parts of destroyed Axis aircraft lay on the ship's deck. Fuel mixed with the seawater, covering the deck; the smell was overpowering; a single spark would set the tanker alight in an almighty blast, taking out the supporting ships with it. The captain noticed that the vessel had sunk considerably more since the previous day. Water pumps on the assisting ships attempted to clear the inundation of seawater, but were not able to clear as much water as was being taken on. The vessel was irreparably damaged, in a crumbling state, descending into the sea. It seemed inevitable that *Ohio* would break apart and sink – and, along with it, the hopes of a nation. But, partway through his grim assessment, the captain made an optimistic declaration; he believed the vessel could stay afloat for another twelve hours as long as the ship did not break in two; and it seemed to be holding together for the time being. There existed the heartbreaking possibility that the tanker would be in full view of the awaiting masses as it sunk. At the captain's seemingly confident call, *Ohio* was reboarded, with many volunteers coming on board for the first time – survivors from other vessels that had been sunk or blown up, that had been picked up by the supporting destroyers; one of the volunteers even had a fractured spine.

Attempts to get the tanker moving resumed; *Rye* towed while *Ledbury* and *Penn* were tied against either side of the back of the tanker to keep it straight and steady. Slow progress was being made. That morning, German bombers attacked the group of vessels tied together; they were unable to manoeuvre and simply had to hope that the bombs would not hit them. A direct hit on *Ohio* would take out the entire group of vessels. The gunners launched an upward volley and deterred the bombers without incident. Just before 11 am, the Luftwaffe returned. Spitfires were present to engage them; however, they were outnumbered. An Axis bomber broke through the air defence and dropped a half-ton bomb; it missed Ohio but landed directly behind it, thrusting the tanker forward, tearing off the rudder completely and creating a further tear in the hull of the ship – and severing all towlines. Incendiary explosives were also dropped but fell short of the tanker. This would be the last Axis attack on the convoy. Despite the further damage, *Ohio* remained afloat; but it was taking in more water, reducing its longevity.

Ohio was sixty kilometres from Malta; the greatest challenge now was to get the deteriorating tanker to port before it became completely submerged, while also navigating the mine fields around the harbour mouth. Attempts were made to get *Ohio* moving again; *Penn* was joined by *Bramham*, pressing against the back of the tanker on the other side, with *Rye* out in front. The pace was slow and steady, just nine kilometres per hour, as the tanker still had a propensity to drift, which carried the danger of nudging a supporting vessel into a mine. Over the next several hours, the group of ships crept their way towards Malta; by evening, the island was in view.

That afternoon, the missing *Brisbane Star* appeared and entered the Grand Harbour with a massive hole in her bow. The missing merchant ship had detoured south towards the Tunisian coast, managing to evade French hostility and enemy bombers to make its way to Malta.

On the dawn of 15 August, the most vital vessel of Operation Pedestal, a dilapidated *Ohio* – shrunk to more than half its height, the middle deck section flush with the water line – limped into the Grand Harbour. Such an enthusiastic reception cheered *Ohio* to port. Canadian fighter pilot Beurling, who had not taken part in the aerial defence of the convoy due to recovering from an illness, nonetheless participated in the celebrations, flying a Spitfire through the Grand

Harbour upside down. Just before 10 am, *Ohio* made it to port and the vital fuel cargo was unloaded in haste. Large pipes were connected to the tanker, pumping out over 10,000 tons of fuel into tanks, the ship sinking lower and lower as the fuel was extracted. *Ohio* finally settled on the bottom of the harbour seabed, resting on its keel, where it broke in two.

Merchant Ship	Estimated Cargo (tons)	Outcome
Empire Hope	14,200	Sunk. Bombed by aircraft, night of 12 August
Clan Ferguson	8,250	Sunk. Bombed by aircraft, night of 12 August
Deucalion	8,960	Sunk. Bombed and torpedoed, night of 12 August
Almeria Lykes	8,960	Sunk. Torpedoed by boat, morning of 13 August
Wairangi	14,560	Sunk. Torpedoed by boat, morning of 13 August
Glenorchy	10,080	Sunk. Torpedoed by boat, morning of 13 August
Santa Elisa	9,520	Sunk. Torpedoed by boat, morning of 13 August
Waimarama	14,560	Sunk. Bombed by aircraft, morning of 13 August
Dorset	8,960	Sunk. Torpedoed by aircraft, night of 13 August
Rochester Castle	7,800	Made it to Malta, evening of 13 August. Damaged by several near misses
Port Chalmers	8,500	Made it to Malta, evening of 13 August. Undamaged
Melbourne Star	12,050	Made it to Malta, evening of 13 August. Relatively undamaged
Brisbane Star	11,050	Made it to Malta, afternoon of 14 August. Damaged, torpedoed by aircraft
Ohio	13,690	Made it to Malta, morning of 15 August. Severly damaged on the brink of being submerged
	151,140	

The vessels and military personnel that participated in Operation Pedestal had endured one of the most violent assaults in maritime history. Over 650 Luftwaffe sorties attacked the convoy over four days; it was immensely outnumbered and at a significant disadvantage on the sea. The tanker *Ohio* endured the majority of attacks and bombardment. It would have taken just one direct hit in the right spot and the tanker, full of fuel, would have created such an immense fire ball – it would have been seen and heard on parts of the mainland continents of Africa and Europe. One direct hit was achieved, but the bomb landed inside the engine room, missing the fuel tanks that mostly comprised the tanker. This was coupled with all the bullets, incendiary devices, bombs, raging fires from damage and planes crashing into the ship. Then, the objective of moving a large and awkward vessel, riddled with holes, cracks, factures and breaks; it is no wonder that the delivery of *Ohio* to Malta is viewed by the people of Malta as a miracle.

Over one-third of merchant supplies initially sent made it to Malta; this was sufficient to sustain the population and prolong the military fight for another two months. *Ohio* delivered eight-five per cent (11,530 tons) of the aviation fuel, diesel, oil and kerosene, losing only 2,160 tons of diesel and kerosene. Overall, the operation had a bittersweet outcome; while the supply rejuvenated the island and bolstered the Allied military fight in the Mediterranean, the losses were great. Aside from the losses of some key vessels, of which the majority of crews were rescued, 457 military personnel lost their lives in the operation. The Maltese people acknowledged the huge sacrifices made for them and their country. The Siege Bell war memorial was built on the site of an anti-aircraft artillery position to commemorate those who had lost their lives. It stands at the furthermost eastern point of Valletta near the entry to the Grand Harbour and features a bronze statue of an unknown soldier laid to rest. It overlooks the harbour where *Ohio* sailed in. The Siege Bell rings daily at midday to commemorate those who lost their lives for Malta.

Malta was the Allies' last foothold in the epicentre of the European war. It is likely the Axis powers would have taken Malta had *Ohio* not ultimately reached the island. The arrival of *Ohio*'s fuel cargo should not be underestimated; this was a defining moment in the war with a positive ripple effect on the Allied campaign throughout the region. It was certainly a defining moment for the nation of Malta.

As expected, *Ohio* was beyond repair. The tanker was moved to another mooring point within the harbour where it was used mostly as storage. In September and October of 1946, the tanker was taken out to sea in two pieces, towed out on separate occasions, about fifteen kilometres north of Valletta, and sunk by gunfire and explosives. *Ohio* was gone but not forgotten. The oil tanker would be held in high regard in the history of maritime great escapes. Remnants of *Ohio* – the name board, steering wheel and flag – are exhibited at Malta's National War Museum in Valletta.

15. Operation Pedestal: The Brisbane Star sails into the Grand Harbour.

16. Operation Pedestal: The sinking tanker Ohio, held up by Navy destroyers, making its way to the mouth of the Grand Harbour, navigating the mine fields. The masts resemble the three crosses on Calvary.

17. Operation Pedestal: The damaged tanker Ohio, supported by Navy destroyers, limping into the Grand Harbour after an epic voyage across the western Mediterranean.

18. Siege Bell War Memorial in Valletta: monument dedicated to those who died during the siege of Malta in the Second World War.

19. The nameboard of Ohio.

FOR GALLANTRY

Journal entry: 13 September 1942

Today, I witnessed the honour of our nation and her peoples being awarded the George Cross Medal. Although it had been months since the official declaration, the medal is now in our presence for the very first time. This tiny island nation, a dot on the world map that lies on the periphery of Europe, is being formally acknowledged because of its resilience and bravery – attributed by one of the most powerful people in the world, the King of England. An unprecedented honour for our nation, a recognition usually awarded only to individuals – Malta's entire population has received one of the British Empire's highest honours. In the eyes of the world, we have become the George Cross Island. This is more than just receiving a medal; it's a symbol of recognition of the suffering and deprivation endured with unwavering perseverance and courage by our people over the past two years. The acknowledgment that our plight is not forgotten, that we are noticed by the Empire – indeed, by the world – for our continued fight for our freedom and the freedom of the world.

Inspiration filled the air like a fragrance, and an encouraging spirit enveloped the gathered crowd. The murmurs of excitement were infectious. The square had been cleared of debris to make it as presentable as possible for the distinguished proceedings to come. Despite the excitement, the reminder of war was ever present, the masses encircled by the crumbled mess of destruction, decrepit and partially standing buildings on all sides. The clambering crowd sought any vantage point available, filling balconies and the tops of buildings, children climbing on mounds of boulders. There was hardly any wiggle room in the byways leading to the square. The threat of attack remained, yet the determined crowd was adamant to witness the honour of such recognition.

The ceremony was hastily put together yet well planned – a small stage setup dressed with the British flag. We even achieved some pomp, not the full splendour that such an honour deserved, but sufficient flair considering the circumstances. The Great British and Maltese flags stood tall, side by side, in the Palace Square: a gratifying symbol of our freedom, that we are yet to be conquered by the enemy.

A hush swept over the crowd as dignitaries stepped forward to the stage. I can't recall the speech word for word, but certain words hit my heart with inspiration and welling pride. 'Island fortress', for example, described the iron will and tenacity of the nation; we stand defiant despite what the enemy throws at us. The phrase 'fight for freedom', encapsulated the reason we have so far endured this war under such dismal circumstances; surrender is the most loathed of all options. We could so easily have given in to end the bombardment and consequent lack of provisions, but collectively we chose the daily struggle of resistance. The word 'gallant' sparked images of spirited bravery and heroic grit: like the many lives sacrificed to ensure that Operation Pedestal was a success, and my dear friend Joe who selflessly gave his life for the nation. At that thought, the accumulation of emotion burst down my face. Joe and gallantry have become synonymous in my mind. Our newly acquired medal is emblazoned aptly with the words 'FOR GALLANTRY'. Whenever I gaze upon the image of the George Cross Medal, I will remember Joe and his gallant sacrifice – as long as I live.

The medal glistened under the sun, encased in a wooden display case. The letter, written by the King's own hand, sits alongside it, on a plinth in the middle of the square. Fenced off and guarded, in case anyone had the itch to grab hold of it. I must admit, when I was in front of it, I myself had an urge to lunge forward. Everyone in attendance filed by to get a glimpse and read the letter for themselves:

a tangible sense of validation for every individual and our nation as a whole.

Sadly, the event was soured by an air raid siren and all dispersed to the nearest cover, ending the proceedings. Amidst the glamour of heroism, reality hit home once again. We're still in the middle of a war, but today will never be forgotten. Malta remains the beating heart, the epicentre of the European war, and the bravery of the Maltese people was acknowledged on the world stage, unlike anything that has ever been bestowed upon any nation. Through the pounding metal hail, in the stranglehold of deprivation, amongst the mounting destruction, the Maltese people will continue to fight on, with award or none, because that is the heart of the nation. That is who we are!

RS

Narrative: September–November 1942

The nation of Malta had been awarded the George Cross Medal by the King of England in April, but due to heavy bombardment at the time, the ceremony was postponed to a safer date. King George VI had a keen interest in Malta and the war efforts that had involved the nation; he was inspired by the people's resolve to resist surrender despite the onslaught of heavy bombardment and severe scarcity; therefore, he declared the order of the George Cross to Malta and its people. British dignitaries brought the medal to Malta and a public ceremony was held in the Palace Square in Valletta. The accolade rewards gallantry and is usually awarded to individuals. It is the second-highest Royal British honour after the Victoria Cross. Via the King's recognition, the Maltese were also acknowledged around the globe – respected throughout the world for their tenacity and determination throughout such an aerial assault never seen before in global warfare. Malta had become a worldwide Allied inspiration and a symbol of the Allied resistance in the Second World War.

The letter, written by the King, was addressed to the Governor of Malta at that time, Sir William Dobbie:

> The Governor, Malta
>
> To honour her brave people I award the George Cross to the Island Fortress of Malta to bear witness to a heroism and devotion that will long be famous in history.
>
> George R.I.
> April 15th, 1942

Sir William Dobbie accepted the award on behalf of the Maltese people and replied to the King, stating, among other things:

... It has greatly encouraged everyone, and all are determined that by God's help Malta will not weaken but endure until victory is won.[6]

By the time of the ceremony, Viscount Gort had been appointed the new Governor of Malta. In his speech, he said:

On my appointment as Governor of Malta I was entrusted to carry the George Cross to this Island Fortress. By command of the King, I now present to the people of Malta and her dependencies the decoration which His Majesty has awarded to them in recognition of the gallant service which they have already rendered in the fight for freedom. How you have withstood for many months the most concentrated bombing attacks in the history of the world is the admiration of all civilised peoples. Your homes and your historic buildings have been destroyed and only their ruins remain as monuments to the hate of a barbarous foe. The Axis Powers have tried again and again to break your spirit but your confidence in the final triumph of the United Nations remains undimmed. What Malta has withstood in the past, without flinching, Malta is determined to endure until the day when the second siege is raised. Battle-scarred George Cross Malta, the sentinel of Empire in the Mediterranean, meanwhile stands firm, undaunted and undismayed, awaiting the time when she can call 'Pass friend, all is well in the Island Fortress'.[7]

---

[6] https://maltagc70.wordpress.com/2022/04/16/
[7] https://maltagc70.wordpress.com/2022/09/13/

To this day, Malta remains the only nation in the world to receive the George Cross. The image of the George Cross Medal was officially added to the national flag on 28 December 1943, where it stands as a testament to the Maltese people's gallantry during the war.

From this time on, the situation on Malta, as well as the Allied fight in the region, improved exponentially. Within weeks of receiving the cargo of Operation Pedestal, Maltese-based offensive strikes resumed to great effect. Air attacks on Axis bases and airfields in Sicily and Libya were met with hardly any resistance. Attacks on Axis supply convoys to North Africa delayed supplies reaching the Afrika Corps. Rommel's opportunity to make a play for Alexandria and Cairo – and ultimately the Suez Canal – was fading. He needed large supplies of ammunition and fuel. An urgent Axis supply convoy was sent at the end of August, which included a tanker carrying 3,000 tons of fuel. Maltese-based aircraft and submarines made haste in attacking the convoy, destroying most of the vessels, including the tanker, which went up in a massive explosion. The prevention of provisions reaching Axis positions in North Africa formed a crushing blow, stagnating their advance and postponing a planned assault on British positions in Egypt. By the start of September, Axis forces began to retreat. The Axis troops in North Africa were now experiencing deprivation, a lack of food and widespread illness. During the months of late August to October, although some supply ships were reaching Axis points in North Africa, over 100,000 tons of Axis supplies were sent to the bottom of the Mediterranean, weakening the Axis campaign in the region, while the British equipped their forces in North Africa.

Several carpet runs were made throughout September and October, delivering further stores and fuel to Malta, including an additional twenty-nine Spitfires. Minesweeping efforts were underway to clear the plethora of mines around the island and create a clearer passage for Allied vessels. Though it seemed the worst of aerial bombardment was over, the Axis powers, namely the Luftwaffe, still held supremacy in the skies over the Mediterranean. The month of September saw less than sixty air raid alerts, nine of those bombing raids. Maltese resistance once again became a thorn in Axis flesh, igniting

Kesselring's rage. He was resolute to stop Malta once and for all. He reasoned that another intense bombardment, as earlier in the year, would again render the island an ineffective Allied base – thus landing the final blow. An all-out assault was planned in October; Kesselring amassed over 650 aircraft across several Sicilian bases. He began his renewed aerial assault just after dawn of 11 October. The attacks were constant; not since the blitz earlier in the year had there been attacks of such intensity. At this point, the island was well stacked with Spitfires but still outnumbered. Squadrons engaged every time the enemy approached, mitigating the destruction and loss experienced by Malta. The aerial onslaught continued for two weeks, the heaviest being in the first three days. The pilots of the RAF were gaining ascendancy; while some Axis aircraft broke through air defences, causing minor harm and damage, the RAF repelled the majority, and the airfields were virtually untouched. In one 60-hour period, approximately 700 aircraft flights were made towards Malta; the RAF destroyed or damaged over 120 Axis aircraft, wiping out almost twenty per cent of the Axis Mediterranean fleet in that time, incurring only minimal losses themselves. The skill and the bravery of the RAF crews on Malta outmatched the Luftwaffe – to the point that, in some instances, they were retreating. Captured German pilots voiced their disdain regarding fighting over Malta; they were exhausted by what seemed an unachievable goal and admitted declining motivation. Coupled with the vast improvements to the Maltese aerial defence, it is unsurprising that by the end of the two-week blitz, more than half of the amassed Axis aircraft had been damaged or destroyed; the RAF lost fewer than forty aircraft. Kesselring's plan had failed. Malta-based attacks were still decimating Axis convoys in the Mediterranean. Kesselring called off the operation and ordered the remaining air fleet to North Africa where the desert war was reaching a critical point. Kesselring conceded defeat; Malta could not be taken; his aspiration to invade had been crushed. The Malta-based air fleet and RAF fighters had gained air superiority over Malta and the Mediterranean once and for all.

At the start of 1941, German radio broadcasts had boasted that Malta would be taken within two weeks. Since the Luftwaffe had begun involvement in their bombing campaign over Malta, the Germans had tried for almost two years to take control of the island. By the end of their Maltese campaign, they were no closer to gaining control over even one square inch of Maltese land. Indeed, Malta could boast, unlike many other nations, that not so much as a single Axis soldier's boot had stepped on Maltese soil.[8]

In North Africa, Rommel and his forces engaged in a back-and-forth battle against the British at El Alamein. By early November, the lack of supplies, personnel and equipment had broken the Axis resistance. Rommel ordered his troops to retreat; however, Hitler ordered Rommel to stand his ground. However, after two days of continuous Allied attack and advance, Rommel had no choice but to retreat. The Allied forces pushed the Axis forces back into Libya and by mid-November, Tobruk had been regained. By the end of the month, Allied troops had reached halfway into Libya. The demise of the Axis forces in the region had spelled the end of the planned invasion of Malta: Operation Herkules was officially terminated. This was the beginning of the end of the Axis campaign throughout North Africa and the Mediterranean. The ongoing failure to capture Malta, largely due to the unyielding determination of the Maltese people – who could have surrendered to end their misery – meant that the Germans were forced to invest additional manpower, weaponry and aircraft in their attempts to take over the obstinate island. This deprived their fight in other areas in the wider war throughout Europe and Africa, lessening their effective advance and military might on those fronts. Hitler had underestimated the Maltese people's resilience and determination to keep fighting. He was convinced that Malta had been subdued once and for all; however, he had misjudged the situation, which emerged as a major blow to his Mediterranean and North African ambitions.

Operation Torch, led by General Dwight D. Eisenhower, the Commander of US forces in Europe, was an Allied operation to land over 100,000 American and British personnel in Morocco and Algeria

---

[8] To clarify, enemy boots did step foot on Malta but only as prisoners of war, not as attacking Axis soldiers. In some instances, enemy soldiers were treated in Maltese hospitals.

to assist the British effort in North Africa. Malta-based aircraft and submarines partook in the operation, launching offensive strikes in Tunisia, Sardinia and Sicily as cover for the safe arrival of the troops. The operation surprised the Germans; they reacted by immediately sending German troops to Tunisia. The French met the initial Allied landings with feigned hostility, publicly protesting while secretly negotiating with the Allies. On 11 November, the French in Morocco and Algeria signed an armistice with the Allies. This frustrated the Germans further; they responded by completely occupying and controlling Vichy France.

20. The George Cross Medal awarded to the island in April 1942.

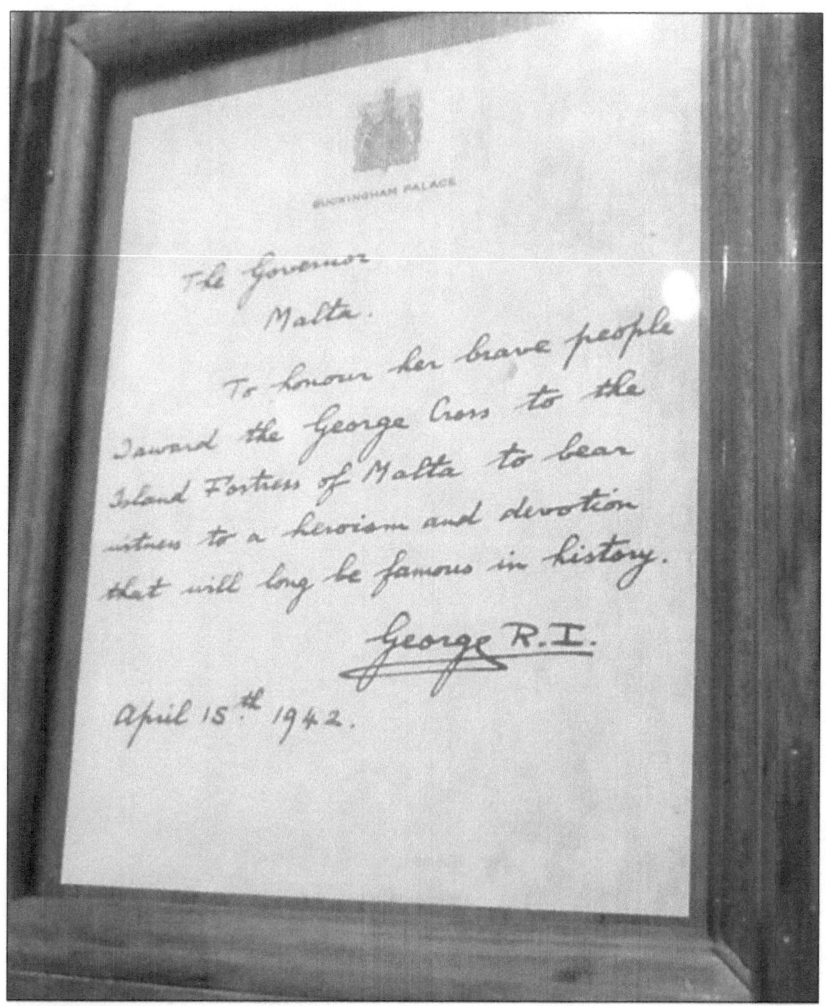

21. The letter written by the King that accompanied the George Cross Medal.

THE TIDE TURNS

Journal entry: 20 December 1942

Words cannot describe how our affliction has dissolved in recent months. A wearisome existence drenched in fear and uncertainty; the nation had deteriorated to a faint pulse, gasping its last breaths. In these days of late, I find myself relishing the sweet fragrance of growing emancipation from the foreboding presence of the Axis war machine; day by day, its overarching shadow recedes from this land. The suffocating smog of Axis aggression has been lifted; a redemptive gust has swept in and rejuvenated the heartbeat of the nation, now breathing freer than we have since the repressive clouds from the north bore upon us over two years ago. Now, another southerly flurry swoops on the shores of western Africa in the form of swarming Yanks, joining the encircling victory trumpets of an impending Allied triumph that has silenced the once-ominous beating Axis drums of North Africa. We no longer fear the sky. The buzz of aircraft overhead once instilled a sense of dread; now the sound is met with cheers and applause from the ground. It is our brave pilots that fly above, dominating the airways like eagles protecting their young, defying the enemy's now pathetic attempts to break through. There is still the occasional air raid siren, but the people take cover as a mere formality as the once-threatening sound has lost its gripping power over us; we re-emerge with laughter and smiles.

The nation has experienced unparalleled despair, merciless bombing that caused immense destruction – it surrounds us like the vast ocean, more buildings destroyed than not; but the people are already making plans to rebuild, some already clearing the way. It's been a nationwide struggle for the basic necessities of existence, and the lingering effects of physical deprivation still remain. Rationing has relaxed but illness and disease continue to harass the ailing; yet they press on, hopeful that life will get better for them. The challenges through which we have persevered have become the foundation of who we are today, upon which has been built an impenetrable resolve, resounding with the sentiment that 'nothing can break us!'

As the year nears its end, there's an increasing air of excitement on two fronts; the island is becoming a mounting hub of military activity, like nothing we've seen before. The scenes instil a sense of security and peace, adding to the excitement of the festive season. Although the day is not yet upon us, it has felt like Christmas every day this month: decorations on display, families making their plans, and even carols being heard much earlier than usual. My heart leaps joyfully at the thought of spending a relieving Christmas with father, mother and our extended family. This will surely be the most memorable Christmas ever, and no air raid siren will dampen our spirit – for the clouds of oppression have been blown away. I know, for many, the lingering sadness of lost loves ones is a constant remembrance, particularly on these special days. The day will never be the same for me; my heart still aches for Joe. Hardly a day passes without thoughts of him. For the first time in two years, I'll be meeting with my dear friends, resuming our traditional Christmas gathering. Last I heard, Louie's mother's bakery had been damaged during the blitz in April (thankfully they weren't there at the time!), Helena had created a makeshift underground classroom for local children, and Maria had joined a women's sewing club, making and repairing dresses. I'm so excited to see them, but no doubt this time our revelry will be replaced with a more solemn tone – it will be the first time without Joe. I didn't want to continue the tradition without him – it didn't feel right without Joe there – but mother made a good point; it's what Joe would have wanted, for us to lean on each other and continue to live our lives together. We were all devastated when we heard about Joe, but no one was surprised by his sacrifice. Our annual Christmas gathering will continue in honour of Joe with a new tradition, a moment to salute and remember our beloved and courageous friend. To my dear Joe, it's almost over, we're going make it through; the tide is turning!

RS

Narrative: December 1942 – January 1943

The might of Malta was building; the island was continually being equipped with military capabilities to become the strongest Allied military post in the Mediterranean and within the British Empire. However, the people had not fared so well. Many were still suffering the ill effects of over two years of daily destruction, deplorable living conditions and constant lack of provisions – with illness and disease becoming more of a threat than bombings. Between the months of November and January, however, several substantial convoys arrived in Malta, encountering minimal resistance. One of the convoys arrived without suffering a single loss, the first since 1941. In all, over 200,000 tons of stores, fuel and various supplies lifted the island out of its desperate state, alleviating famine and the declined health of the nation. The improved situation in the Mediterranean and relative safety of convoy passage meant that the submarine carpet runs – which had served the nation well over the years – would come to an end; the island's longevity seemed assured. Axis air attacks continued but were swiftly diminishing; from over 150 in October to thirty in November and only five in February.

The British Parliament acknowledged the role that Malta had played in the Allies' ascendancy in North Africa. It was stated that 'Malta has been one of the determining factors in the struggle for the conquest of North Africa, and we are particularly proud of the great contribution that it has made'.[9] Indeed, Hitler's hopes of capturing the Middle Eastern oil fields had been completely dashed by the Allies' success in pushing the Axis forces out of Egypt – taking over 35,000 German and Italian prisoners along the way – while German troops stagnated in the Caucasus region.

In January, Churchill and Roosevelt met in Casablanca, Morocco; they agreed to several strategic commitments going forward – building up American troops in the European arena, a combined bombing offensive on Germany, and invading Sicily and subsequently Italy – in which Malta would play a key role, leading to an unconditional surrender of the Axis powers.

---

[9] Mr Robert Richards, MP for Wrexham, House of Commons, 19 November 1942.

The Axis stronghold was incrementally being repelled from the region. By January, British troops had taken Tripoli, while the Americans approached from the west in a joint effort to corner Axis troops in Tunisia. By February, British troops from the east and US troops from the west had entered Tunisia and closed in on the remaining Axis resistance in the northern half of Tunisia.

Elsewhere, fatigued German troops were ordered to hold their positions on Russian fronts to begin a counteroffensive; however, they were weary from the bitter winter and not as well equipped as the Soviets to endure the inclement weather. By early 1943, the Soviets were gaining the upper hand, either prompting German troops to surrender or pushing them back, relieving key cities such as Moscow and Stalingrad, as well as in the Caucasus region. On mainland Europe, the Allies begin a bombing campaign on Germany that would last throughout the year. Previously, in the Pacific arena, the Japanese empire had occupied lands housing twenty per cent of the world's population. The USA, however, had begun to repel the Japanese, capturing several islands in the southern Pacific, as well as liberating Papua New Guinea, with the help of Australian troops; the Japanese eventually abandoned the island.

END IN SIGHT

Journal entry: 25 April 1943

There was an observable magnificence about today's spring day, perhaps made all the more potent by the nationwide celebration of Resurrection Sunday. Having just heard the story of darkness being defeated, when I stepped out of church this morning, I felt I was entering a new beginning on this once-battered land that had languished, seemingly in the depths of hell. When the sunbeams fell across my face, I was seized by the moment, basking in the caressing warmth. The last two spring seasons had been consumed by a prolonged and bitter winter. The clear blue sky had become a faded memory; a dark dust haze shadowed the land, depriving all living things of regenerating sunlight. The ground riddled with crumbled stones and explosive-tilled soil, a colourless landscape – Malta could only be seen through a lens of black, white and grey. The lingering fragrance of smoulder, fine dust and explosive fumes conquered every breath of air. The harbour waters were a cesspool of greasy contamination. But now the miserable gloom has subsided and the waves of spring wash over this land like a soothing balm. How spectacular it is! Where once I took it for granted, I now indulge in every nuance of the beauty brought by this season. The clouds have parted to reveal the pure blue, and unhindered rays of sunshine. The sparkling light glistens on the waters once again. The foul stench of war has been carried away by the refreshing sea breeze, complemented by the charming scents of seasonal flowers in our fields that paint the nation anew with splashes of colour. Yellow daisies stand tall side by side, dancing in accord in the gentle wind. The snapdragon's vibrant pink commands attention; equally mesmerising is the wild red of a gang of poppies that grace the fields; they complement each other so beautifully against a cloudless light blue background – it's truly breathtaking. My lungs are revived by the purity of nature's breath, untainted by the noxious fumes of destruction. I've heard it said that you don't appreciate what you have until it's taken away from you, and I now understand how true that is. The precious nature of peace is something for which I will be daily grateful. I've come to value the seemingly insignificant moments of everyday life, such as the morning stretch after a good night's sleep, the first comforting mouthful of a delectable home-cooked meal, a serene stroll down my street without a care on my mind.

This most sacred day of our nation is the first Easter in two years not celebrated under the clouds of bombardment. The events of Easter appropriately symbolise the events in Malta over the last few years. Jesus spent three days in the confining gloom; it seemed that the mighty adversary had won and could not be overcome. But out of the apparent impossibility burst new life and victory over the powerful forces of darkness. Similarly, Malta and her people have spent three years living under an oppressive shadow. The nation was beaten down, deprived and starved, on the precipice of taking its final gasps. The likelihood of overcoming such an indomitable foe was in the realm of improbability – a seemingly forgone conclusion. Then, there came extraordinary turns of events; and the nation was revived. A resurgence reminiscent of Jesus' resurrection – defying and overcoming a much mightier foe to make it through the darkest period in the history of this nation, stronger than ever before!

It's been a demanding season for my people; in the bleakest moments, it seemed it would never end. But a new dawn beckons, ushering in a new season unlike all previous dawns. There's an unmistakable strength about this new season. It signals the close of what was the most gruelling period ever known to the Maltese people. And although the war is not yet officially over, the Allied tidal wave is gaining momentum, sweeping up from the south with the potency of the rising sun, shining its light over the Mediterranean and onto mainland Europe; with each passing day, the brightness intensifies, casting a greater shadow on the enemy forces, making it ever clearer that the end is in sight.

RS

Narrative: February–June 1943

Axis forces in North Africa were starved of supplies due to the success of Malta-based strikes on Axis supply convoys. Air and submarine attacks sunk over 200 Axis vessels in the opening months of 1943. Rommel left North Africa and returned to Germany due to his failing health and morale. Towards the end of April, Axis forces were cornered in the northern part of Tunisia. The Allies eventually captured the capital, Tunis, and Axis forces surrendered on 13 May; approximately 250,000 German and Italian troops were taken as prisoners. The war in North Africa was officially over; the Allies had solidified their supremacy in the southern Mediterranean. Hitler had lost a key front in his plans for world domination. He ordered the remaining Luftwaffe fleets in North Africa to the USSR to aid his weakening position there, where German troops were being pushed back on several fronts.

Now that the Allies had secured the region south of Malta, the offensive effort would turn towards the north. In the following weeks of the Axis surrender in North Africa, Malta would be replenished with more fighter planes, naval vessels, landing craft, vehicles, tanks, military provisions and military personnel: preparation for the planned Allied invasion of Sicily, Operation Husky. The island had become an impressive military base teeming with some of the finest aircraft and powerful naval vessels in the world. The streets were lined with all types of military vehicles and every available spot in the Grand Harbour and ports around the country were filled with naval vessels. Three new airfields were built to contain the bursting number of aircraft – over 600 – constructed within a month. Engineers deemed that the best and most resourceful method of creating landing strips would be to connect existing roads, clearing the surrounding path; Malta now resembled a giant unsinkable aircraft carrier. Certainly, a different scene to when Malta first entered the war some three years earlier, beginning with only a few outdated biplanes still packed in crates. Now, this island minnow – once considered indefensible, the worst Allied military post in Europe – had become the most powerful Allied military base in Europe outside Britain. Malta was the staging post of one of the most important Allied military offensives of the Second World War, hosting top military brass: the Allied Naval Commander, the Allied Air Commander and Supreme Commander of the Allied forces in Europe – Dwight D. Eisenhower. Even the King was keen to visit Malta, eventually making his way there in June.

In the months leading up to Operation Husky, the Allies prepared well for a successful invasion of Sicily. Aside from amassing military arsenal on Malta, offensive air strikes were conducted on Axis bases throughout the region. The Axis bases of Pantelleria and Lampedusa, in close proximity to Malta, were neutralised. Additionally, a clever ruse was devised to deceive Axis intelligence. Axis forces knew of an imminent southern invasion by the Allies and had been increasing the number of aircraft and troops in Sicily, but were unsure of the when, where and how. In Operation Mincemeat, the Allies dressed a corpse in full Royal Marine uniform and released the body from a submarine near the coast of Spain. A briefcase was attached to the corpse with documents outlining an Allied invasion of Sardinia and Greece. The Spanish authorities passed this information to the Germans. Hitler believed that this was the location of the imminent Allied invasion and diverted resources from Sicily to Sardinia and Greece in preparation for the invasion. Thus, the Allies had successfully convinced Hitler that the invasion would occur elsewhere. Even after Allied troops landed in Sicily, the Axis powers held to the belief that Sardinia and Greece were to be the main points of invasion.

The Lascaris War Rooms would be the epicentre of Operation Husky, one of the largest amphibious invasions in world history, launched from one of the smallest nations in Europe. Over 150,000 military personnel, predominantly British, American and Canadian troops, embarked for the land invasion of Sicily. They first landed on 10 July, and over the next few days, more than 3,000 sea vessels and 4,000 aircraft would take part in the operation, launching from the main hub of Malta, as well as Allied bases in Tunisia, Algeria and Egypt.

TINY BRIGHT FLAME

Journal entry: 8 September 1943

I'm overjoyed beyond words. I feel as though, for the first time since war broke over this land, I'm breathing without restraint, each new breath refreshing my soul, reviving a new spirit within, liberating dreams and possibilities that were once held captive in the dungeons of hopelessness. It's a surreal moment, that at times seemed inconceivable; but today, the sky has parted to reveal a new canopy over this nation. It's official; Malta has come through the most gruelling period in its long history! This once besieged nation, on the cusp of annihilation, ever pressed beneath the belligerent's thumb, has finally overcome oppression. The aggressors have been subdued and lay at the mercy of the ever-increasing Allied powers. We, the Maltese, held on! In the end, it was they who surrendered, not us. What was the most vulnerable piece of land in the region has proved its worth. I like to think of Malta as the diamond of the Mediterranean, indeed of all Europe. Just like the tough diamond is formed through intense pressure, our nation has been made endurably resilient through the tribulations of recent years. A diamond is small yet contains great value; as declared by leaders around the world, Malta, a tiny island, showed itself invaluable to the overall fight against tyranny, and through it all, shined as a beacon of light amidst the overwhelming darkness.

It's ticked passed one in the morning and there's not a hint of the festivities winding down. Hardly a soul is sleeping, but unlike previous years when bombardment and uncertainty kept us awake, tonight the uncontainable delight and celebration won't allow our bodies to rest. Once-hoarded wine is shared freely around, such a stash begging to be brought out at such a time. It's heartening to see the elation of my townspeople, released from the burden of war. Although the bombs long fell silent, great relief envelopes the heart, knowing that the threat is completely eliminated – even more satisfying, we know we didn't bow to the enemy's intimidation. I can almost hear the nation's collective sigh of liberation amidst the jubilation; the laugher, singing and dancing fill the air as a pleasant aroma: an uncontrollable flow of joy radiating on faces as they chant, 'it's over, it's over!'

I write these words perched on the fore steps of the Basilica, taking a momentary break from the revelry. I look up at the night sky, admiring the lively sparkles dotting the outstretched blanket of deep blue, in a state of liberty for the first time in three years. I gaze upon the towering columns I rest beneath and the impressive dome of the Basilica. Every time I'm here or walk by, I'm reminded of the moment I was metres away from a half-ton beast that tore through the roof like paper and shook the building as if it were built on sand. It still gives me goosebumps to this day. This church shouldn't be standing here intact; yet it does. It stands defiant as a testament of the hope, faith and spirit of the people.

Thinking about how we made it to this point; in huge part, this is due to the brave and gallant people who selflessly sacrificed their lives; they are engraved on the soul of this nation for eternity. One especially will always remain close to my heart; when he comes to mind, I instinctively look upward … Oh! As I did that just now, a shooting star streaked across the sky in the blink of an eye. We did it Joe, we are free! I recall the day at the beach, just before the war began. It was the last time we were all together as a group. We were children, teenagers, at the time, unaware of the intensely demanding period we were about to enter. Through the challenges and hardships, we grew into adults, well beyond our age suggests. Then there are others, like Joe, who have come through this war as ageless heroes.

The main reason we celebrate this victorious day is not because we had more advanced weaponry or machines, not because we had more military men; neither were we mightier than they. On the contrary, we were constantly belittled in the shadow of the enemy's military power. We live in triumph today, yes, because of the sacrifice of others and the one greater, more powerful attribute that we the Maltese people had, that they didn't … heart! This is what kept this nation, once deemed indefensible … unconquerable!

RS

Narrative: July 1943 onwards

In the dawn of 20 July, the 3,340th air raid siren sounded over Malta, followed by a brief bombardment. Little did the population know, this was the last air raid warning and attempted bombardment of the island.

The invasion and Allied occupation of Sicily was swift; within three days, over 150,000 Allied troops were onshore; towns and cities had been taken and thousands of Italian soldiers had surrendered. The Italian people's resentment towards Mussolini increased. The Fascist Grand Council removed military control from Mussolini's hands and, by the end of July, he was deposed, arrested and taken into captivity at a mountain fortress by a new Italian government. Operation Husky was successfully completed on 17 August; Sicily was fully under Allied control. The new Italian government sought an armistice with the Allies. The unconditional surrender of Italy was announced on 8 September; one of the major three Axis powers had been neutralised. The Maltese Command declared, 'the Italian battle fleet now lies at the anchor under the guns of the fortress of Malta'.[10] The Allies prepared for an invasion of mainland Italy with the cooperation of the Italians, but Hitler was not going to cede Italy without a fight. On the 12th, Hitler sent commandos to rescue Mussolini and bring him to Berlin where he was given authority to lead the Italian Socialist Republic of northern Italy. Hitler ordered German troops to Italy to continue the fight and halt the Allied invasion.

In November, Churchill visited Malta; and in the following month, the President of the USA, Franklin D. Roosevelt, also arrived on Malta where he wrote a letter to the Maltese people:

> In the name of the people of the United States of America, I salute the Island of Malta, its people and defenders, who, in the cause of freedom and justice and decency throughout the world, have

---

[10] https://timesofmalta.com/article/malta-s-role-in-the-surrender-of-the-italian-battle-fleet-to-the.503402#

rendered valorous service far above and beyond the call of duty.

Under repeated fire from the skies, Malta stood alone, but unafraid in the center of the sea, one tiny bright flame in the darkness — a beacon of hope for the clearer days which have come.

Malta's bright story of human fortitude and courage will be read by posterity with wonder and with gratitude through all the ages.

What was done in this Island maintains the highest traditions of gallant men and women who from the beginning of time have lived and died to preserve civilization for all mankind.

Franklin D. Roosevelt, December 7, 1943[11]

The war continued to rage throughout mainland Europe and the Pacific, the Germans remaining obstinate in their desire for world supremacy. However, the Allies made significant gains and by the beginning of 1944, they had control of southern Italy and the Soviets were pushing the Germans back towards Germany. In June, the Germans retreated from their base in Rome; on the 6th, over 155,000 Allied troops invaded France through the region of Normandy: the operation otherwise known as D-Day. In the second half of the year, Bulgaria and Romania — once allies of Germany — declared war on Germany. The Allies liberated Paris and Belgium. The Hungarians turned their back on Germany, signing an armistice with the USSR; however, the Germans continued to fight in Hungary. In February 1945, Churchill and Roosevelt met in Malta to discuss the

---

[11]

https://missionsforeign.gov.mt/en/Embassies/Me_United_States/Documents/Roosevelt.pdf

final campaign against the Germans. In the following months, the German resistance was defeated in Hungary and Allied troops entered Germany. In April, President Roosevelt suddenly succumbed to an illness and passed away; he was replaced by Vice-President Harry Truman. The Allies continued to make their way up through Italy, reaching Bologna in the north. The Soviets took Vienna and advanced towards Berlin from the east, while the Allies continued their march from the west. Berlin was encircled by Allied and Soviet troops. High-ranking German officials, Hermann Goering and Heinrich Himmler, were dismissed by Hitler: Himmler for seeking an armistice with the Allies. The last three days of April were eventful. On the 28th, Mussolini attempted to flee to Switzerland but was captured by Italian partisans and executed. On the 29th, German officials, without Hitler's approval, agreed to an unconditional surrender. On the 30th, Hitler – fearful of the besieging Soviets and Allies charging towards Berlin – hiding in his underground bunker, where he had been since January, committed suicide. What Hitler caused the Maltese people to endure – forcing them underground and into a squalid, despairing existence – he himself ultimately endured, forced underground to live in fear. But unlike the Maltese people, who re-emerged to the surface to face their reality with courage and determination, Hitler remained underground where his life ended in cowardice.

The war in Europe was over; the Allies declared victory in Europe on 8 May 1945. The date is commemorated throughout Europe to this day, known as 'Victory in Europe' (VE) Day.

Conflict continued in the Pacific arena, where the Americans were heavily involved. It was a gruelling campaign of jungle warfare. In August 1945, the Americans dropped atomic bombs on Hiroshima and Nagasaki. Japan formally surrendered on 2 September 1945. Finally, after six years and one day, the Second World War was officially over.

∞

The war over Malta officially ended the day Italy surrendered. The Maltese people had suffered devastation unlike that experienced by any other country during the Second World War; no other civilian population endured a greater aerial siege, one of the most aggressive in warfare history. It was a merciless bombing campaign aimed to isolate and pulverise the island into surrender, lasting over three years and two months. Malta endured over 73,150 sorties, over 2,350 hours under air raids and over 15,000 tons of bombs released; 6,700 tons were dropped within a six-week period between March and April 1942. To put this into perspective, within an eight-month period, 12,000 tons were dropped on London in total, which is five times the size of Malta. By the end of the war, Malta had become the most bombed country in the world. Today, it remains the most bombed country in Europe; and although other nations have suffered a greater tonnage of bombs in subsequent years, Malta remains the most bombed country in the world in terms of bombs per square metre. Approximately 7,500 military personnel perished for the cause of Malta, and 1,581 civilians lost their lives. The underground shelters proved crucial in keeping casualty rates low. Over 30,000 buildings were damaged or destroyed, leaving 50,000 people homeless, almost twenty per cent of the population.

The successful defence of Malta was one of the key strategic wins that aided the Allied victory in Europe in the Second World War. The European war was fought on three major fronts: northern, eastern and southern. The victory of the southern front relied heavily on who controlled Malta; as the evidence showed, whomever held control of the island was the dominant force in the region. The Axis powers lost their supremacy in the Mediterranean and North Africa due to their failure to gain ultimate control of Malta. A regression in the order of events reveals the source of the Allied success of the southern front: the invasion of mainland Italy, the invasion of Sicily, the complete takeover of North Africa, the control of supply routes in the Mediterranean – all flow from Malta remaining under Allied control. Had the Axis powers gained control of Malta, they would have enjoyed unfettered access throughout the Mediterranean, crushing all Allied attempts to move about in the region. They would have built up sufficient resources to overwhelm the Allied forces in North Africa, taking Egypt and the Suez Canal, cutting Britain off from India and Australia. Eventually, they would have acquired the prized Middle Eastern oil fields, which would have supplied the Axis war machine with an endless supply of fuel to fortify its fight against the Soviet and Allied forces.

The tenacity of the Maltese people was a major factor in the island's longevity. Granted, the British military assisted with military capabilities and the overall fight, but without the people's support, undying will to never surrender, and unusually high morale in deplorable circumstances, the British may not have lasted as long as they did on the island. The unwavering Maltese resistance exposed the ineptitude of the Italians, which in turn forced the Germans to intervene. Troops and resources were taken from other fronts in the USSR and North Africa, weakening Axis positions in those areas.

During the time of bombardment, the bravery of the Maltese people was recognised on a global scale – they became a symbol of hope for Europe and, indeed, the world. This small island nation showed incredible grit and resilience through utter obliteration, resolute in resisting a much mightier foe when other, larger and better equipped nations had capitulated to the same enemy. Malta remained the only country in Europe targeted by the Axis forces not to have been invaded or to have ceded an inch of territory to the Axis powers. Even the British were invaded and lost the Channel Island territories of Guernsey and Jersey.

The story of Malta's heroic stance stands shoulder to shoulder with other remarkable stories and events of the Second World War. In every moment of the war, Malta was always outnumbered, always fought against the odds, and was always overpowered – yet, it was never defeated. It is unfortunate that the story of Malta is not widely known and sits in the shadow of other notable Second World War stories. A word or a phrase such as Dunkirk, D-Day, the Battle of the Bulge, can spark immediate recollection of valiant acts and amazing outcomes. It would not be out of place to add another term to that list: Island Fortress.

EPILOGUE

In the years following the war, Rita and her friends remained in close contact, their bond strengthened by the loss of their beloved friend Joe. Every year on the anniversary of his selfless act, they gather at the place, on Fort St. Elmo, where he was immortalised, and raise a toast to Joe's memory.

Maria met a wealthy British Lance Corporal who served in Malta during the war. They married and went on to split their time between England and Malta. Her husband even fulfilled her dream, buying a modest holiday house on the shores of the French Riviera. True to her word, she invited her friends to her thirtieth birthday party at the holiday house and covering their travel expenses.

Helena's desire to become a teacher would eventually be realised. During the war, she continued to teach the younger children, concerned about their educational welfare in their formative years. She took the initiative to create a makeshift child-friendly space in the underground shelter, including a small library of books she had gathered. The children would continue to learn despite the enormous disruptions and this distracted them from focusing only on the war. She was lauded for her efforts and promptly initiated as a teacher at the local school. She quickly gained the esteem of her peers and rose through the ranks; within six years, she was promoted to headmistress.

During the war, Louie and his mother had worked the majority of their days baking as much bread as possible to feed the starving masses, until their bakery was destroyed during an intense night raid in April 1942. His mother, getting on in years, decided against starting another business but encouraged Louie to open his own bakery, promising to assist him. Eighteen months after the close of the war, he opened his bakery, *Louie's Treats*, one of only three bakeries at that time in all Malta. He soon gained a reputation for making the best pastizzi in the land, and Rita was a frequent customer.

When the war ended in Malta, Rita's role at the Command Headquarters had changed to that of assisting the administrator of planning and development – to begin rebuilding the nation. An innate uncertainty lingered within, however, regarding her place in a seemingly new world, living in a postwar nation. She discovered that many of her countrymen felt the same way. The war experience had had a profound impact on her life, and she recognised a change in her attitudes, beliefs and values, reshaped by a sense of moral certainty – that good and evil indeed both exist in this fragile world.

The war had ended but it was not an easy time for the people. Yet, despite needing to reconstruct their homes and livelihoods, they remained grateful and optimistic for the future. Even following the war, the people of Malta continued to be a source of inspiration to Rita; she was motivated by their determination to rebuild with the little they had. She wanted to give back to the people of Malta – because she had derived such inspiration from them over the years – the best way she knew how: through the written word. At just after midnight, on 11 June 1945, she wrote her daily journal entry as a letter addressing the Maltese people. The only way she knew to have it read by the people was to drop it off at the *Times of Malta* office in the early hours of the day, in the hope that the editors would find it worthy of publication in that day's newspaper.

Journal entry: 11 June 1945

To the gallant people of Malta,

On this five-year anniversary of the belligerent first strike on our land, we remember the day that commenced the history-defining moment of our nation. Peace abruptly departed as the land's foundation quaked. Aggressive thunders shook the firmament; pieces of sky tumbled down in rage. The clear blue heavens obstructed by a low-lying dust canopy, casting a dim shadow and blanketing the entire island. The pristine Mediterranean air infected with the breath of destruction on the wind. It began as a nightmare; what was hoped to be short-lived turned into a daily reality for years to come. Day after day, wave after wave, aggression swept over us with unrelenting force. The will of the Maltese people never more challenged. The resilience of the nation never more tested. We walked through the valley depths, hounded by dark shadows of torment, towering on all sides. We were at the whim of the aggressor: thrown into the lion's den, thrust into the fiery furnace, beaten down by the cyclonic gales. The worst that was feared to come, did indeed come ... but we made it through the darkest valley with steadfast resolve. They destroyed our buildings but we will rebuild. They destroyed our houses but we will create new homes. They thwarted our way of life but never deterred our determination. We outlasted their bombs, we outlasted their attacks, we outlasted their attempts to break us and we outlasted them as a people! We, the Maltese are still here; the Axis natives have disappeared. We were outnumbered, overpowered, plagued, besieged, exhausted, starved, worn-out, grief-stricken ... yet, we prevailed. Malta was never taken, though much larger nations with greater military power and larger populations were. We did not concede a morsel of territory; my dear people, wear that satisfaction as a badge of honour!

The remnants of grief and struggle will linger for many; the loss of livelihoods and of heartbreak, lost loved ones. Such pain will endure until our minds can remember no more, a permanent scar on the heart I know all too well. Know that you are not alone. Together we faced the most oppressive powers that threatened our freedom and values. Together we suffered severe want and the direst of circumstances, and together we will re-establish our lives and heal our nation. I have learned that each new day brings with it a new hope, underpinned by the uplifting deep faith of the nation. I once lived under a perpetual dark cloud of gloom that saw no end. But hope was always there, just like the sun still shines in all its strength behind the seemingly immovable dense clouds, awaiting the moment the burdensome darkness parts just enough for the slightest sliver of light to pierce through, illuminating the smallest promise of better days to come.

To the ageless heroes of this land and the lands that fought with us and for us. Words are not sufficient to express our gratitude for what you gave for this land and her people. You are immortally etched in the heart of Malta, remembered for posterity. Your life for our freedom; a selfless act that is embroidered in the fabric of our nation. We may not have met, we may not know your name, but we know of your courage and we will be forever in awe of your sacrifice.

It has been just over one month since the war ended in Europe. The war continues to rage on the other side of the world but is reaching its inevitable end. An absolute victory to the Allies; the forces of good triumphed over the forces of darkness. Who would have thought that the smallest country involved in this war would become the biggest source of hope for Europe — and the world. Once considered the most vulnerable piece of land possessed by the Allies, Malta has proved itself to be an impenetrable fortress.

What has made us a fortress? Is it the solid rock on which our nation rests? The naturally carved harbour? The high cliffs and rocky shallow shores to deter enemies? Yes, these natural attributes helped; but they are not what made us endure. I know why we, a crumb of land, engulfed by the shadow of a vicious giant, were able to resist and withstand the assault of the world's most foreboding enemy. I saw it and lived amongst it. It was our granite perseverance — to never give in to the exceedingly powerful tyrant! It was the faith to persist despite the overwhelming impossibility! It was the fortitude to remain in the fight for as long as our breaths sustained us! And while our bodies may have faded due to the lack, our hearts beat strong as one: a collective tune of 'never surrender!' That is what made us a fortress! That is why Malta, forever the minnow in this battle between David and Goliath, overcame insurmountable circumstances. Despite the glaring chasm of might and power, we refused to stand down. We stood our ground and, although knocked to our knees more than once, we got up each time. The overwhelming darkness attempted to consume this tiny flickering flame, kept alive by the spirit of the Maltese. Unbeknownst to us, the eyes of the world were watching this little light dwarfed by the encroaching gloom. A speck of darkness cannot exist in the light, but a pinpoint of light can exist in vast darkness — and that is what Malta became to the world as it dwindled in the abysmal depths. Malta became a symbol of hope and enduring resistance in devastating times. The spirit of our nation reverberated throughout the Mediterranean, to the ends of the earth, inspiring our friends; and no doubt, still felt to the detriment of our foes. This enduring spirit is neither spoken of nor written on parchment for all to read; rather, it is seen in the lives of the people. The world saw the Maltese fight on, they saw the Maltese never surrendering, and they saw the Maltese rise up from the ashes to be victorious. Take a bow, my brave countrymen, the world applauses. Dignitaries, from Prime Ministers to Presidents and Kings, laud our resistance and determination to remain resolute in the face of such want and suffering. They acknowledge that without the tenacity of the Maltese to endure, the war would still be raging in Europe. Take heart people, know that your plight was not in vain; we played a part in ending this war for good and restoring harmony in Europe – and the world.

The reach to grab arms will be replaced with the outstretched arms of peace, the whistle of dropping ornaments replaced with the chirps of sparrows, the march of tyranny replaced with the dance of freedom. Peace, world peace. Then we can truly exhale the words the world's soul has been gasping to breathe. It is finally over! It is YOU, my dear Maltese people, the galvanised and unyielding heart of us all, that makes our nation an island fortress. Indeed, the island fortress of the free world.

Rita Schembri
11 June 1945

Rita's open letter to the nation was published on the front page of the *Times of Malta* on the five-year anniversary of Malta's entry into the war and just over one month after the war ending in Europe. The response to her letter was unprecedented; the news outlet received hundreds of letters of admiration in response to her uplifting and encouraging words; the page was pinned on community boards and glued on the walls of buildings throughout the country for all to read. The *Times of Malta* acknowledged her writing prowess and immediately offered her the position of editor of national affairs ... she accepted.

Bibliography

Online Sources

77 Years On: Understanding the Significance of the Santa Marija Convoy.
https://www.um.edu.mt/library/oar/bitstream/123456789/51581/1/77_years_on.PDF

Allied Invasion of Sicily.
https://en.wikipedia.org/wiki/Allied_invasion_of_Sicily

Everyone is Starving Here | The Siege of Malta.
https://blog.forceswarrecords.com/everyone-is-starving-here-the-siege-of-malta/

Forgotten Fights: Malta's Faith, Hope, and Charity, 1940.
https://www.nationalww2museum.org/war/articles/british-biplanes-faith-hope-charity-1940

George Beurling. https://en.wikipedia.org/wiki/George_Beurling

Great Siege of Malta.
https://en.wikipedia.org/wiki/Great_Siege_of_Malta

How Malta Survived the Second World War.
https://www.iwm.org.uk/history/how-malta-survived-the-second-world-war

Islands of Malta: World War Two.
https://www.youtube.com/watch?v=gUhT6JADZ3I

Italy's First Attack on Malta in WWII.
https://timesofmalta.com/article/italys-first-attack-on-malta-in-wwii.796860

Malta and World War Two.
https://www.historylearningsite.co.uk/world-war-two/war-in-the-mediterranean-sea/malta-and-world-war-two/

Malta Campaign. https://ww2db.com/battle_spec.php?battle_id=94

Malta Convoys. https://en.wikipedia.org/wiki/Malta_convoys

Malta Convoys. https://navymuseum.co.nz/explore/by-themes/world-war-two-by-themes/malta-convoys/

Malta: War Diary. https://maltagc70.wordpress.com/

Ohio: The Ship that Refused to Sink – How an Oil Tanker Saved Malta. https://www.youtube.com/watch?v=baJBXE63M1w

Operation Husky: The Allied Invasion of Sicily. https://www.nationalww2museum.org/war/articles/operation-husky-allied-invasion-sicily

Operation Pedestal – The Mission to Save Malta. https://navalhistoria.com/pedestal/

Operation Pedestal. https://en.wikipedia.org/wiki/Operation_Pedestal

Operation Pedestal: Facts and Figures About Those Fateful Days in August 1942. https://timesofmalta.com/article/operation-pedestal-facts-figures-fateful-days-august-1942.1049152

Operation Pedestal: The Convoy that Saved Malta. https://www.youtube.com/watch?v=0inR2jRW_P8

Operation Pedestal: The Rescue of Malta. https://warfarehistorynetwork.com/article/operation-pedestal-the-rescue-of-malta/

Operational Pedestal. https://war-experience.org/events/operation-pedestal/

S.S. Ohio and the Siege of Malta. https://www.youtube.com/watch?v=MbMwo8gBks0

Siege of Malta (World War II). https://en.wikipedia.org/wiki/Siege_of_Malta_(World_War_II)

Siege of Malta WW2. https://www.timetoast.com/timelines/siege-of-malta-ww2

Surviving The Siege of Malta | Battlefield Mysteries | Timeline. https://www.youtube.com/watch?v=tOKwANmj_n0

The Illustrious Blitz. https://www.independent.com.mt/articles/2021-01-17/newspaper-lifestyleculture/The-Illustrious-Blitz-6736230162

The Most Bombed Place on Earth – Operation Herkules vs. the Undefeated WW2 Island. https://www.youtube.com/watch?v=HzK-aVvgQ4g

The Resupply of Malta in World War II. https://www.jstor.org/stable/44642105?seq=1

The Siege of Malta in World War Two.
https://www.bbc.co.uk/history/worldwars/wwtwo/siege_malta_01
.shtml

The Siege of Malta in WWII: Holding On to the Island Fortress.
https://warfarehistorynetwork.com/article/the-siege-of-malta-
holding-on-to-the-island-fortress/

The Siege of Malta WWII.
https://www.youtube.com/watch?v=KIR8TA2pBUg

The World War Two Siege of Malta in Numbers.
https://www.independent.com.mt/articles/2020-05-31/newspaper-
lifestyleculture/The-World-War-Two-Siege-of-Malta-in-numbers-
6736223694?fbclid=IwAR0COLQlRAlicrGl0CKQrW_qkuC1aw
ryWRHeiHNLbM7patvcWWL5sbiIJb8

Timeline of Events 1941–1945.
https://www.historyplace.com/unitedstates/pacificwar/timeline.ht
m

Visit the CWGC in Malta and Explore Malta's History.
https://www.cwgc.org/visit-us/visit-malta/

World War II Database.
https://ww2db.com/battle_spec.php?battle_id=94

WW2 People's War. https://www.independent.com.mt/articles/2021-
01-17/newspaper-lifestyleculture/The-Illustrious-Blitz-
6736230162

WWII The Siege of Malta.
https://www.youtube.com/watch?v=qFi8BkcJCZc

Book Sources

Hastings, Max. (2021). *Operation Pedestal: The Fleet that Battled to Malta 1942*. Harper.

Holland, James. (2004). *Fortress Malta: An Island Under Siege 1940–1943*. W&N.

Jordan, David. (2013). *A Chronology of World War II: A Day-By-Day History of the Biggest Conflict of the 20th Century*. Amber Books.

Shaw, Antony. (2002). *World War II: Day by Day*. Lifetime
    Distributers
Willmott, H. P., Charles Messenger and Robin Cross. (2012). *World
    War II*. Dorling Kindersley.

www.poete.com.au/books

https://books2read.com/IslandFortress

All books by Peter Tonna available at book outlets around the world